SOLD TO THE MOUNTAIN MAN

COURAGE COUNTY CURVES

MIA BRODY

1

TRACE

I SURVEY THE OLD RUST BUCKET FILLED WITH JUNK. There's a lot of scrap metal inside of it—small appliances like toasters and TVs, metal pet cages, auto parts, and old electronics litter the vehicle that was towed up my mountain today. Even the car itself could be broken down for scrap.

Normally, this sort of haul is a dream come true for me since I'm a metal welder, creating complex art pieces for businesses and collectors alike. But the three men who brought it up here aren't my regular sellers. No, there's something shifty about these guys that has my teeth on edge.

"How much did you say you wanted for all the junk in this heap?" I ask even though I already have a rough idea of the figure they'll name.

The man in the gray beanie, the one that seems to be in charge of the whole operation, names a figure that's too low. Obviously, he's not used to selling scrap and judging by the way he and his friends keep twitching, the profits from this little venture are going straight up their noses.

I step around to the back of the trunk, keeping my face carefully blank. My hip is acting up today, but I refuse to let it show. If I don't show the pain, it doesn't exist. A mantra that a scared boy learned too early in life.

"You want it or not?" He asks, rubbing at his face.

Fuck, the three of them are practically vibrating. For a split second, I consider letting this opportunity pass me by. I don't need trouble, especially the trouble that comes from addicts who are just looking for their next high. But something compels me to reach for the car again. I don't want to let it go even though I don't understand why.

I pop the unlocked trunk and peer into it. There's even more scrap metal in the back, various rusted tools, a tire that's clearly deflated, and blonde hair. My gaze follows the silky gold and though I have to squint, I finally see it. A hypnotic blue gaze staring back at me.

It's hard to tell under all the dirt, but there's a

woman back here. Her heart-shaped face and big, blue eyes give her an innocent look. She has the plumpest, most kissable lips I've ever seen.

"Please," she mouths the single word and my heart breaks right here. Just what the hell has she been through? What led her to hide in the back of this car? Was she hoping that wherever she was headed was better than where she'd been?

I slam the trunk before Gray Beanie can get too close. I turn to the three men. "New term. I want the whole car and everything in it."

The guys look at each other in confusion before the one in an orange tracksuit says, "It'll be more money."

I cross my arms over my chest, trying to ignore the tightness in my stomach. Is she OK? Does she have enough oxygen? How long has she been in there?

Gray Beanie scratches his arm. If he keeps going that hard, he'll hit bone soon. "Yeah, double the price."

I snort. I'd gladly pay triple what they're asking, and I have it to spare. My creations caught the eye of eccentric millionaires early on and I've been well compensated for my work. But I'm a simple man. I don't need millions upon millions so most of my earnings are quietly funneled toward a charity for abused kids.

Still, I don't have extra cash on me, and there's no way in hell I'm leaving her alone while I retrieve more money. Instead, I take a gamble that they're pretty damn desperate for that next high. I toss the pouch with the money I do have. "Take it or leave it."

Gray Beanie starts counting it while his friends anxiously nudge him, encouraging him to just accept it. Yeah, they're already thinking about the good times they're about to have. He stops counting the cash to glance at me. "I can get more cars, you know."

"This was a one-time deal," I growl at him. There's no way in hell I want his kind of trouble up here again. "Now get the fuck off my mountain."

I don't have to tell them twice. Orange suit quickly unhitches the car, and the three of them are shoving their way into the tiny pickup truck they used to tow the junker up here in the first place.

I watch the truck until it's just a speck on the horizon. "Good riddance, motherfuckers."

That's when it hits me what I just did. I did more than buy a rust bucket that was probably stolen to begin with. I just bought myself a woman.

Hurrying to the trunk, I pop the hood again. I

peer into the dark and part of me expects her to be gone. Maybe I've been on this damn mountain for a very long time. Maybe I'm pretty damn lonely, especially as I've spent the past few months watching my friends get married.

But she's not a figment of my imagination.

The woman is still there.

She stares at me with wide eyes, still not moving a muscle. Just how terrified is she? What was so horrible in her life that she had to leave it all behind and take a chance with strangers?

"I'm not going to hurt you," I promise, thinking of a sixteen-year-old boy who ran from his own living nightmare. I mean for my voice to come out soft and reassuring, but living by myself for over twenty years means I'm not good with people. I don't know how to comfort and soothe anyone.

She probably can't get out because of all this junk so I grab the deflated tire and toss it on the ground at my feet. A rusted toolbox is next followed by a microwave. Damn, how did she get in here?

I work in silence that's interrupted only by my own grunts. The midday humidity causes sweat to roll down my skin, and I can't even blame it on the sun with this cloudy weather promising thunderstorms soon.

Most of this stuff in the trunk is unusable. But it doesn't matter if I don't use any of this car or what was inside of it. Because she's here, and something crazy in me is saying she's meant to be here.

The woman isn't saying anything. She watches me. Her gaze unnerves me, makes something hot rush through my body that has nothing to do with the humid day. There's something in her that I recognize even though I can't explain it.

When I'm done, I reach for her arm to help her out.

But she shrinks away, somehow managing to fold even more of her body into the back. The trunk is deep enough that I'd damn near have to climb in if I wanted to scoop her out.

I think of the time I spent on the streets, of how I quickly learned that people can't be trusted. "It's OK if you're in trouble. I won't let anybody hurt you now."

She still makes no move to leave.

Not that I expected her to. Any idiot can make her a promise and she's smart enough to know that. A new thought occurs to me. Maybe she knew the morons from earlier. "Did you know those guys that were here? Did they hurt you?"

White hot rage unfurls in me at the thought. No

one will ever put their hands on her again. I won't let them. I'll die to protect her even though I don't understand why.

She shakes her head, the first time she's communicated since she mouthed a single word earlier. It's not much but it feels like progress.

Her stomach growls.

"I got food in my cabin," I bark, pointing to my cabin with my thumb. It's through the clearing, about a hundred feet behind me.

No answer.

Part of me debates just reaching in and hauling her out anyway. She's got beautiful curves but she's no match for my size. I'm already big and years of bending metal to my will—forcing it into shape—has strengthened me. But for some reason, I don't drag her out.

I want her to come to me.

To not be scared of me.

Princess would know what to do. I'm an old grump, but Princess will comfort her. With a decisive nod, I turn back to my cabin and retrieve my kitty.

I have to pause before we go outside to slather her in sunscreen and put her little floppy sunhat on. She makes a mournful sound, humiliated at having to wear it. But even with the overcast weather, the UV rays are still a threat.

"Just convince her to trust us," I explain to Princess as I carry her outside.

I set her in the trunk and watch. Despite disliking people as much as I do, Princess goes right up to the runaway.

The woman holds out her hand to Princess who sniffs her before allowing herself to be petted. I watch her hand stroke my cat's soft fur, studying it. Her nails are neat and trimmed, painted a pretty red color that tells me she hasn't been in this rough situation for too long. Something about the realization makes the tightness in my chest ease.

"What's her name?" The question is so quiet that I almost miss it.

"Princess," I answer. Not terribly original for a cat but she looked like a little princess to me. "Do you want to tell me yours now?"

She hesitates before finally whispering, "Molly."

2

MOLLY

"MOLLY," THE BEARDED MOUNTAIN MAN IN FRONT OF me growls my name softly. The way he says it makes me think it tastes sweet on his lips which is a weird thought to have about him. He looks big and gruff and has wrinkles that drag his mouth down in a permanent scowl. Yet he's been gentle with me, gentle with his cat.

I'm used to men that are calculating, that will say and do whatever they want to get you to trust them. Only to plunge the knife deep into your back later. Everything about him might be an act.

But the dark gray clouds above rumble out a warning. It doesn't matter if he's worse than my father and his friends seeing as I don't have much choice. I can't stay in this car all day. As it was, I didn't mean to fall asleep in the back of the old clunker.

"What's yours?" I ask, my voice coming out hoarse. I don't remember the last time I had a sip of water or a bathroom break. My legs are cramped, and I'm desperate to leave this trunk that reeks of burned rubber and wet carpet.

"Trace," he answers.

Princess purrs softly as if confirming that the man can be trusted. She's a white cat with ice blue eyes under that floppy hat. Her coat is thick and healthy even if she's covered in some type of lotion that smells like sunscreen. Her weight is normal. There are no signs of mistreatment that I can spot. That has to mean he's a kind man, right?

Thunder cracks the skies again and lightning flashes, making my decision for me. "Is your place close?"

I think it has to be if he just showed up with the cat. I try to remember how long he was gone, but I have a headache from not eating and I'm more than a little dizzy. When was the last time I had a meal? Had to have been a couple of days ago.

He grunts and I'm assuming that was an affirmation. He holds out his hand again, but he doesn't reach for me the way he did earlier. He's making it clear that I have a choice this time.

I study his hand, unsure of why it feels like everything is about to change. It's a big, calloused hand. Burn scars dot the backs. The thought of him being injured makes my stomach feel funny.

Finally with a deep breath, I take his hand. Electricity dances along my skin and it has nothing to do with the thick, humid air. I let him help me out of the trunk, stumbling on my feet since my legs are asleep from being cramped up for so long.

His hands go around my hips for a brief second before he instantly drops them. I feel bereft without his touch, and I don't understand it. He looks away from me and points to a clearing in the trees.

Princess sits at his feet and meows. He picks her up and holds her close to his chest. There's something about seeing him carry the cat in his big arms that makes me melt a little inside.

I take a moment to get my bearings. We're in the middle of a forest, somewhere on a mountain. The air here smells fresh and clean, and the promise of rain hangs heavy.

"Do you like it here?" I ask as I start walking beside him. He limps with every step he takes. I noticed it earlier too when he went to grab his cat.

Sometimes when I get nervous, I start to babble. "I mean, of course, you like it here. You live here. Most people like where they live, I guess. I never did, but maybe I would have if—"

He stops walking so fast that I stumble on my feet again.

I pause to right myself and crane my neck up to stare at him. He has sky blue eyes that look like the perfect summer day. One of those endless ones with no clouds in it and a cool breeze.

"Are you in legal trouble?" He grunts out.

I snort which is clearly the wrong response. But my father kept me under lock and key my whole life. He'd promised I could go to college when I turned nineteen. Like everything else he said, it was a lie.

He rubs his beard and studies me. The big mountain man seems just as curious about me as I am about him. But the difference is while he has nothing to hide, there are a whole lot of things that I have to hide. At least, I do if I hope to survive. "So, if I call the sheriff there will be no warrants out for your arrest?"

"No! You can't do that." The moment my identity is logged in an official report somewhere, my father will know. He'll send someone to retrieve me, and I'd rather die than go back.

Trace looks up at the sky as if he's searching for something. No heavenly voice thunders back at him, telling him what to do with me.

I expect him to tell me to go, that I'm too much trouble.

The silence between us continues to stretch and I'm desperate to fill it. "I'm an excellent housekeeper. I can clean and cook and sew." All skills that would make me a good little wife, skills that were preparing me for a life that would be hell on earth.

He grunts and begins limping back to his cabin. But he doesn't say I have to leave so I figure that it's OK if I go with him.

"I'm no trouble," I promise. "I'll just have a good meal and be on my way. I don't even need anything fancy. Not that I would object to a good lasagna right now. That's like the best comfort food there is. I mean, pasta and cheese. It just doesn't get better than—"

He stops walking again.

"Right. Maybe you just have some peanut butter sandwiches. Those are good too." He's frowning at me. I haven't even gotten to his cabin yet and I've already overstayed my welcome. I'm not very good at this runaway stuff. "I'll take anything you'd give me, and I'll be quiet too."

That last part seems to satisfy him, and he nods as if we've come to some agreement. It figures I'd leave home only to run to another man who just wants me to be seen and not heard. Not that it matters. Clearly, I'm not staying with him. I'm just crashing in his cabin for a couple of hours. Get some food, maybe use the toilet.

I open my mouth to tell him that I'll be out of here soon when I spot the cabin. It's a real log cabin, right here in the middle of the forest. A puff of smoke is coming from the chimney and the windows are lit up with light from the inside. It looks like the place is welcoming me and for some crazy reason, I feel like I've found home. Something in me aches at the realization.

The porch is messy and cluttered, but not dirty. It just has various appliances stacked around, like the mountain man can't be bothered to go through it all.

"Why do you have so much stuff? Are you one of those people that digs through trash and finds price-less antiques and sells them? That would explain why you were buying that car. But there was nothing valuable inside of it, trust me. I know valu-able things."

I realize I'm talking again and shut up. He's

already made it clear that he doesn't want me interrupting his peace and quiet.

He steps inside the cabin. It's just as messy and cluttered as the outside. But as I survey it, I begin to see a pattern of tiny groupings. I think he's sorting the items though it's hard for me to figure out exactly what they have in common. It all seems random to me. Maybe he's grouping it by how much money he can get for the things.

"Bathroom," he grunts and leads me down a small hall that's also cluttered with more things. The space is even smaller when I'm trailing after him. His shoulders are so big and broad. Everything about the man is and for some reason, that makes me feel safe.

Unlike the rest of the house, the bathroom isn't cluttered, and I use the toilet quickly. When I go to wash my hands, I frown at my reflection in the mirror. I'm covered in grime, and my long hair looks matted and wild. Not like the princess I'm supposed to be.

There's a linen closet beside the huge glass shower stall. I debate taking a shower but decide against it since I'd just have to put my dirty clothes back on again. So instead, I grab some washcloths and do my best to clean myself. I wash my face and braid my hair, fighting another wave of dizziness.

I scrunch my toes in the beat-up sneakers I'm wearing that are too tight. As soon as I was out of New York, I stopped at a thrift store and ditched my designer outfit. No point in calling attention to myself.

When I'm done, I search the bathroom. I'm looking for proof of a wife or girlfriend. The man may lack communication skills, but he's attractive in that rugged way. More than that, he's kind with big hands. I don't know what it is about them. I've never paid too much attention to anyone's hands.

Before I can muse about that, there's a faint scratching sound at the door. I finally give up my stealthy search that has revealed nothing more than the fact that the guy owns a shampoo-conditioner-body-wash combo. Clearly, the man is not one for extravagance.

Princess bumps into the doorframe then pauses and takes a step back. After a second, she strolls in and heads for the litter box.

I leave to find my mountain man, wandering again through the piles of stuff. Maybe he's not one of those online sellers. Maybe he's a hoarder and the things comfort him. The thought that he's surrounded by things and not people makes me sad for him.

Moving through the living room, I follow my nose. He's cooking something. Something that smells better than the gas station hotdog I had three days ago.

He turns when he hears me in the kitchen and points to the stove, looking like a kid who just completed his first solo art project. "Lasagna."

The floor dips and I sway just as the lights go out.

3
TRACE

"FUCK," I GROWL THE WORD AS I STEP FORWARD, JUST managing to catch the curvy woman as she lunges for the floor. Is she hurt? What if she's been shot or beaten or worse? The thought has me panicking. Not much scares me these days but the thought of someone hurting this precious woman puts a knot of fear in my gut.

I pull her close and survey my options. The kitchen table is too hard, and I can't even get to my couch anymore. I've been meaning to clean the place up and move my scrap metal out to the workshop. But well, it's not like I ever have company. If you don't count the runaway I'm holding in my arms.

It feels right to be holding her even though I

know I don't deserve the small comfort. I've never sheltered or protected anyone. It's not in my genes. The only thing flowing through my veins is pure evil. I can't let myself hurt her. Just the thought makes me feel like I can't breathe.

When I get to my room, a space that's just as cluttered, I put her on the bed. It takes superhuman strength to let her go. I already want to own her, to possess her. I'm a sick fuck. That's why the moment she's well, I'll send her on her way.

The minutes tick by slowly as I wait for her to regain consciousness. I just want to see those blue eyes again. I need to know if she's OK.

I consider undressing her long enough to check for injuries but then I don't. No, what I need to do is call Cash. He's the town doctor, and he'll tell me how to help her.

With shaking fingers, I unlock my phone. I'm about to dial him when she stirs. She makes a soft, pained noise. My heart hurts when I hear it.

I take a step closer to the bed and start to touch her only to drop my hand. I don't know why I want to touch her. All I know is that I do. I want to feel her skin against mine, always. I want to be connected with her in every way. "Easy."

She gives me a scowl of her own, but I can't help chuckling. It's so damn adorable. Just like when Princess gets mad at me, there's no real venom in it. "How did I get here?"

"You were hiding out in a car." Shit, maybe she has a head injury. It's time for Cash to evaluate her even if I hate the idea of him talking with her or examining her or hell, just looking at her. Maybe I'll blindfold the fucker first. Doesn't matter that the man is happily married with kids of his own. "You may have hit your head today. I'll call the doc—"

She sits up fast, those beautiful blue eyes wide with panic. "Don't. No medical help."

No cops and no medical attention. She's in deep shit. It was something I knew already but this only confirms it.

A smart man would send her on her way, but one look at her and I can't do that. I have to fix this for her. I have to set her free from the monster that put the terrified look in her eyes. "You have to tell me what we're up against."

She starts to shake her head then stops. Instead, she lifts her chin in a move of defiance. "I just want a hot meal then I'll be gone."

I think about my life before, about how important it was to be in control. I can give her that for now. I can let her think she's in control. Then once she trusts me, I'll figure out what has her running scared. I'll demolish the threat and then...well, I don't know what comes after that. She leaves, I guess. Even as I think the thought, something in me snarls at it.

There's a beast inside that wants to own her, possess her. He's telling me that I bought her. But he's a screwed-up fucker, so I don't listen to him. Instead, I do my best to give her a reassuring smile. Actually, I think I just bare my teeth. It's been a long time since I've attempted a smile. "Come on. I'll get you some water."

She tries to stand again but wobbles on her feet.

Dammit, I'm not going to watch her struggle. I don't ever want to see her struggle. There's something in me that can't stand it. Scooping her into my arms, I carry her back to the kitchen and help her sit on a chair.

I fill a glass of water and watch her gulp it down. As soon as she's done, I fill it again. She takes smaller sips this time, watching me as I watch her.

When she finally puts it down on the table, I drop to my knees in front of the chair. I brush her hair back from her face and inspect her. My gaze roams over her as I try to unlock all of her secrets. "How old are you?"

"I'm legal. How old are you?" She answers in a tone that's way too casual.

I grip her chin in my hand. Her skin is soft and smooth. "That's not what I asked."

She rolls her eyes. "Nineteen. Happy?"

I search her face, trying to discover if she's telling the truth. But nothing else she's said has been untruthful. So far, she's just dodged questions. She hasn't outright lied to me.

The timer beeps to let me know the lasagna is done. I drop my hand and rise to my feet, ignoring the way my hip and knee protests. The thing about having a fucked-up hip is that eventually it fucks up all the other joints that are busy compensating for it.

"How old are you?" She asks.

Old enough to be her father. Old enough to know better than to put my dirty hands on someone so pure and sweet and innocent.

Despite the tough girl act she's trying to put on, I see through it. My little runaway is scared and over-whelmed. She's in desperate need of a protector, and I'm the warrior willing to fight hell itself for her.

I plate her food and place it on the table before I

take a seat across from her. I try to think of something to say but years of silence with only Princess for company hasn't made me a great conversationalist. But that's OK because Molly fills the quiet after a few moments.

"This is so good. How did you learn to cook like this? I can cook some. I tend to burn things which isn't my fault. I get distracted with my clay. It's hard when you have something you love that just completely absorbs you, isn't it? I mean, real life is hard and I'd rather live inside my creations."

I nod at what she's saying. When I'm welding, time loses all meaning. There's only me and the heat and the twisting of the metal. Still, it's not lost on me that she said real life is hard. She's using her art to escape, a feeling I've known all too well.

I wait for her to go on, to tell me more about her work. When she doesn't, I frown and finally ask, "What do you do with the clay?"

Her face lights up. She looks so damn happy that I've responded. "I'm making a fairy village. I started with just the fairies then I thought they needed a place to live and now..." Her voice trails off. She shrugs like it doesn't hurt before continuing, "It doesn't matter, I guess. I left them behind."

I want to reach out and take her hand. I want to

offer her physical comfort. My body aches to do that, my arm tingling with the need to touch her. But I refuse to allow myself to move toward her. "I left everything behind when I ran away too."

4
MOLLY

HE COULD BE TELLING ME THE TRUTH. HE COULD BE
playing a game, trying to get me to slip up and reveal
where I come from. But I can't risk that. No doubt
my father would pay good money to get me back.

We drift into silence again and I fight the over-
whelming urge to start talking. I don't like silence.
It's loud and oppressive and so cruel, like being left
alone to grow up in a big house. It's why I started
making my clay creations. My designs were something to talk to and with the fairy village, I felt like I
had friends. It's a stupid thought that has me
blinking back tears.

I finish my food and push to my feet. "Thank
you."

"You don't have anything on you," Trace says, still sitting.

I lost my backpack with a few scant supplies at a gas station. I was distracted by that damn hotdog. "I'm traveling light."

"And broke," he points out.

"So?" I can feel my body tightening. Here I thought he was a nice guy. I thought he was kind. Guess that's just further proof that I'm a stupid, naive girl.

"Want to earn some cash before you go?"

I can't believe I put myself in this situation. I went to some strange man's cabin. He's twice my size and he could easily overpower me. But then if he planned to hurt me, why didn't he do it when I fainted earlier? It doesn't make sense for him to wait until I'm conscious and can fight back. "I'm not going to suck your dick."

He looks like I've slapped him but quickly recovers, his face going blank again. Maybe he wasn't thinking about that at all. "I could use some help moving this junk to my workshop. It's a mile or two down the road."

"You're going to pay me to help you move your stuff?" I repeat, studying the man. "You're bigger than me. You could move all of this easily."

"Hip is acting up," he grits out, like it physically pains him to acknowledge his weakness in front of me. "It'll take me twice as long to get it done by myself."

"What happened to it?" I ask. I know you're not supposed to ask people about injuries and medical conditions. But I can't help being curious about Trace.

He waves it away, clearly not taking offense to my question. "Horse riding accident as a kid. I got bucked. Never got medical attention so it healed wrong."

"Well, what's in your workshop? I thought there was something about serial killers moving you to a second location, and it's been a shitty week. But I don't want to end up murdered because I trusted the wrong person."

"But you'll hide in the back of a car driven by three addicts," he answers.

"Yeah, I know it was a dumb decision. You don't have to point it out. But I didn't know they were crackheads which leads me to think that I don't know if you're a serial killer."

He wipes a hand down his face like he finds me utterly exhausting. He wouldn't be the first person, but the gesture still pierces my heart all the same.

"My point is just that one bad decision in the past shouldn't keep me from making good decisions now. Also, I was tired and didn't mean to fall asleep. I was getting out the next time they stopped at a gas station."

He pulls his phone from the table and punches something into it then he passes me the device. I accept it and scan an article with his picture next to it. He's a master welder that's been commissioned by a mall owned in Asheville. He does something called gas metal arc welding. I don't even know what that is, but it sounds cool.

I chew on my lip and return the phone to him. Earning some money would be nice. Getting to spend a little more time around the mountain man would be even nicer. "That doesn't sound like a serial killer's biography."

"We work hard to be normal nowadays," he drawls. One side of his mouth quirks up in an almost smile.

I nod and survey the house. "Might take a few hours. Why do you keep this stuff here if you have a workshop somewhere else?"

"Donations. People donate their old shit and I haul it back up here. Look through it and toss out what I can't use."

He doesn't appear to have done much tossing out of things. Still, I don't think I should needle him about that. Instead, I say, "So the piles are sorted by..."

"Types of metal. Some types aren't useful for welding. Some are," he answers and finally gets to his feet. There's the briefest flicker of pain in his eyes, and I hate that. I hate that he hurts, but I turn away. He's like me in some ways, too proud for anyone's pity.

We spend the next three hours loading the back of his truck with junk, and we've barely made a dent in the messy house. It's all useless stuff to me but he looks at it the same way I look at clay. With a gleam in his eyes, like he's imagining all the things it could be.

By the time we're done, my t-shirt is hot and sticky. The sky overhead still promises rain, but it hasn't delivered it yet.

Trace and I cover the bed of the pickup with a tarp, tying it down. I ignore the way the muscles in my arms protest from the hard work I've been doing. It's worth it to spend a little more time with this man.

"You said the workshop is only a couple miles down the road?" I ask to confirm after Trace has tossed me a water bottle. I drain it, thankful I'm no longer dizzy like I was earlier today. A good home-cooked meal and a few glasses of water have made me feel so much better. Or maybe it's just being around Trace and feeling so safe.

Princess struts onto the porch without her floppy hat. She stares at Trace.

"Don't you be looking at me like that," he grumps.

She meows mournfully.

"Alright, you can go." He opens the truck door, and she scampers inside quickly.

I join her, taking the passenger side of the bench seat. The truck is at least forty years old judging by the vintage radio. But I kind of love the vehicle. It fits Trace.

He leans across the seat and for a second, I think he's going to help me with my seatbelt. But instead, he reaches into the glovebox and yanks out sunscreen and a purple floppy hat. He takes a second to apply the lotion before placing the hat on her head.

He explains to me, "She's at very high risk of sunburn and skin cancer because she's albino."

"Is that why she's so pink everywhere?" I noticed earlier her nose and ears are a shade of soft pink that I've never seen on a cat before.

She curls up next to Trace's thigh. She's on the seat between us, purring in complete contentment.

He starts the truck and reaches for the stick shift. His big hand grasps it with ease. His biceps bulge as he works the shaft. "Yeah, and her depth perception is off. Sometimes, she runs into things. She's a happy girl other than that."

I'd be a happy girl if I had someone like Trace looking out for me too.

Classical music starts playing from the speakers and Trace says, "Watch this."

He flips the station to one that plays today's hits, and his cat meows. First once then a second time. She grows louder with each meow until it sounds like she's singing along with the pop song. He flips it back to classical music and she instantly quiets.

He chuckles, the sound a soft rumble in the cozy truck cab. "She does it with every station but this one. Apparently, my girl likes Chopin and Liszt."

I laugh. "You have a cat with an ear for classical music."

He pulls to a stop in front of another log cabin. Only this one is a lot bigger but still just as pretty. Excitement bubbles up in me as I realize where we are. "Is this your workshop?"

He grunts in agreement. "I'll show you around before we unload."

I follow him into the workshop after he unlocks the door and disarms the security system. Several large worktables are arranged in various sections of the warehouse over the concrete floors. Tools and safety gear are carefully hung on the walls. But it's the beautiful statue in one corner that causes my breath to catch in my throat.

The shiny metal gleams in the light as I get closer. At first glance, it's just a nude woman, but the more I look at it, the more I see the hidden message. She's not just a woman. She's a dragon, fierce and powerful and mighty.

"You're an artist," I breathe, now fully understanding what he does. "You're an artist like me."

5
TRACE

YOU'RE AN ARTIST LIKE ME.

When she says the words, pride fills my chest. We're alike in this. More than that, she likes what I make. I can't explain why I made that piece. It's entirely different from anything else I've ever created.

More than that, I've never been able to part with it. I just couldn't bring myself to sell it. Now I think I know why. I wasn't making that for anyone else. I was designing it for her. She is the strong woman with a fierce dragon inside. I just have to get her to see that.

She glances at me, a question in her gaze.

I nod, giving her permission.

With trembling fingers, she reaches for the statue

and runs her fingertips across the metal surface. Seeing her hands on my art has my cock lengthening and my breath coming in desperate pants.

The beast in me wants her hands on me that way. I want her rubbing my skin and murmuring those little nothings under her breath. Would she do that? Touch me if she understood what I am? Who I am?

I've tried to atone for where I come from, but it'll never be enough. Men like me are dangerous. We deserve to be locked up. The best thing I can do is keep my distance from the pretty little thing in my workshop. Even knowing that, I find myself moving close to her, standing behind her.

My whole body is aching with the need to touch her, to wrap that long pretty braid around my fist and tug her head back so I can press kisses to the column of her throat.

I've been alone for decades without touching someone, without getting touched in return. Somewhere along the way, I convinced myself that it didn't hurt. That being isolated didn't leave me aching at night, wishing I had someone to come home to.

But this woman right here, she's making it hard for me to believe those things. She's making me ache for a different future. One that she's a part of.

She turns around and nearly bumps into me. She makes a soft squeak of surprise.

"You're beautiful," I murmur, dropping my head and angling close to her. I can feel her breath against my lips, see the way her pupils have grown wide.

She's panting, sucking in deep breaths. It would only take a slight movement from her, and I'd close the distance. I'd kiss her like I've been dying to do since she showed up at my place.

But I can't be the one to make that move. Not after what she said earlier about not sucking my dick. I don't want her to think for a minute that's what I'm after. Well, I don't want her to think that's the *only* thing I'm after. Truth is, I want to protect her, slay her demons, then carry her back to my bed.

Something clatters on the floor behind us, and she nearly jumps out of her skin.

I turn to see Princess chasing a green anole, a type of lizard common to the area, around the workshop floor. She looks like she's having a grand time while the poor fellow is running for his life. "Princess, stop tormenting the guy."

My words don't deter my cat from her mission, and I glance back at Molly. Her cheeks are flushed, and she's avoiding my gaze. Damn, I really read that shit wrong. She doesn't like me.

I shove down the disappointment and go to distract Princess. At least, I can keep one of us from causing trouble.

It takes another three hours to unload all the junk from the back of my truck and put it in the storage area of my workshop. By the time we're finished, it's nearly dark.

She doesn't need to be wandering the mountains alone at night. Courage County is safe. It's mother nature I'm concerned about. The thunder continues to sound, teasing us with the possibilities of storms.

"Why don't you crash at my place tonight? Then you can leave in the morning," I say as I glance between my truck and the darkening sky.

Something flickers across her features, but it's gone before I can tell what it is. "Yeah, in the morning."

"Unless..." I start then stop myself. There's no way she wants to stay with me for longer. I've already made her uncomfortable once. I won't do it again tonight.

"Unless?" She prompts.

There's hope in her gaze. I know I haven't mistaken it. That's what gives me the courage to say, "Unless you helped me out with my place. Cleaned out the junk with me, maybe give it a bit of a makeover. You said you were good at the house-keeping stuff. I'd pay you for all of it."

My heart is about to pound out of my chest by the time I stop talking. There's easily a week's worth of things she could do around my cabin, and the thought of getting her to spend another seven days with me is irresistible. Actually, I want her to spend all of her days with me. But that's not on the table. No way will she go for that, so I offer myself the next best thing. A taste of what life would be like with another person, with her specifically. A woman that feels like mine.

"But you're still not a serial killer?" She asks. "Because at this point, I'd be really disappointed in you. I sort of consider you my friend. My first real friend. Sorry, that's lame."

My first real friend. Something about the statement hits me in the gut. I think my girl has spent her life just as lonely as I have. I can't think of that. It makes my chest hurt too much to imagine her alone and sad. Instead, I quirk an eyebrow. "You'd be disappointed in me?"

She puts her hands on those thick hips and nods again, looking so damn cute. "Extremely."

"Then I'll try to repress my darker urges." I meant to tease her, but my voice comes out too deep and too growly. I remind the beast in me to calm the fuck down.

I open her truck door now that we've settled our agreement, and she climbs inside. Maybe it's my imagination but I think I hear her mutter under her breath that I shouldn't repress all of my urges. But that's just my stupid heart hoping for something I'm never going to get.

"You're sure about giving me first shower?" She asks again as I shove a clean set of clothes at her.

After some reheated lasagna for dinner, her eyes are drooping, and she looks like she's about one second from hitting the floor. But then she asked if she could use the shower after me.

"I might take all the hot water, and I most likely won't even say sorry because I'm pretty grimy and it's been such a long day," she explains all in one breath before biting down on that plump lip again. I want to see it wrapped around my cock, want to feel her teeth graze along my shaft.

Since I can't say anything that's not filthy, I just nod at her request and gesture toward the bathroom.

As soon as she's gone, tucked away from me, I

breathe a sigh of relief. But then the water starts, and I think about her standing naked under the spray. Think about her rubbing my shower gel all over those perfect tits.

Fuck, I can't focus on stuff like this.

I move to my front porch and breathe in the mountain air. I try to let it untangle all the thoughts in my head but it's not working tonight. I need to distract myself.

Reaching for my phone, I start a group call with Roman, Blade, and Rafe. The three of them live on the mountain, the same as me. They're my friends along with Brennon and Nash who are both happily married now. Lucky bastards.

"I'm not going hiking with you fuckers," Blade says, answering the call. He lost his arm a couple years back and moved to the mountain recently. He doesn't talk much about himself, and I've never asked.

"It's not about that," I answer. "I got a woman here."

Rafe's voice comes on the line next. He sounds perturbed. Like Blade, he's a newer addition to our crew. "Well, then what the fuck are you doing talking to us?"

I don't want to hear Rafe talking about the things

I should be doing with my curvy little runaway. I
don't want him thinking about her like that. "She's in
trouble."

"You want me to look it up, figure out what's
going on?" Roman runs a construction company.
He's served time and has a network of contacts. If
anyone could figure this out it would be him.

I want her to come to me. I want her to trust me.
"Not yet. Give me some time."

"We'll keep an eye on things then," Roman says,
already knowing where my mind was going. "I'll
spread the word around the mountain. Make sure
she's covered."

Some of the tightness in my gut eases at his
words. I can trust my friends to have her back
without hesitation. Knowing Roman, he'll have
patrols organized within an hour. They'll be moni-
toring my land and keeping an eye out for unexpected visitors.

"Appreciate it," I tell them before saying my
goodbyes.

Now that I know my friends will be watching
over her with me, I can focus on gaining her trust
and learning her secrets. Then I'll destroy whoever
has her so afraid with my bare hands.

6
MOLLY

I FINALLY FEEL CLEAN, AND I SMELL LIKE TRACE'S shower gel, which is weirdly comforting. I never thought smelling like a man would be nice but then again, I smell like the guy who rescued me from what could have turned into a horrible situation.

I thought earlier in his workshop that maybe he wanted to kiss me. I thought that was why he was so close and invading my space. But then he didn't, and I felt embarrassed and humiliated. He has to be close to twenty years older than me. He probably just sees me as some kid running away from home.

Shaking off the thoughts, I remind myself not to make this weird for him. The longer I can stay here and earn a few dollars, the better it'll be when I finally have to go.

I shrug into his t-shirt, the thin material rasping against my nipples. What would it be like to have Trace's hands on them? What would his lips feel like on my body? Just the thought has me tingling all over.

I leave the bathroom in a puff of humid air and step into Trace's bedroom. He's turning down the sheets and he straightens when he sees me.

"You take the bed tonight." He nods then slips past me into the bathroom. He shuts the door and the sound of the lock clicking annoys me for some reason. Not like I'm going to come bursting in after him.

"Big, bossy mountain man," I huff as I get into the Alaskan king bed. It's large enough that five of me could comfortably sleep in it. Except that sleep doesn't come easy. I stare up at the ceiling in the room that's illuminated with a bedside lamp.

Something scrapes against the windowpane and my heart pounds. For a second, I fear my father's men have found me. But then the noise sounds again, and I realize it's just branches scraping along the windowpane in the storm.

Shaking my head at my anxious thoughts, I do that breathing exercise I learned in a meditation video. I try to imagine myself walking through a forest. I close my eyes and count sheep. Nothing works and I find myself listening to the sound of the shower water.

Trace is in there, the water running over his body. It's a very nice one if that t-shirt he wore today is any indication. It got sticky with sweat and plastered to him, outlining his six-pack and toned pecs. I imagine touching his chest, pressing my curves against him. Would he like that or would he push me away in disgust?

It's thoughts of Trace that calm me. He's here with me. I'm safe.

Still, I wait until the shower water shuts off before I turn off the lamp beside the bed. The darkness only makes me curious about Trace and his isolated life here in the mountains.

He opens the bathroom door, light from behind outlining him. He looks like an angel. My big, bearded angel that rescued me.

"You're still awake," he grunts. "Thought you'd be asleep by now."

"It's weird sleeping in such a big bed," I admit. How come it doesn't remind him of how alone he is? Or maybe it does, and he likes that. "Where are you going to sleep?"

"Living room," he grunts the words.

"The lumpy couch doesn't look particularly comfortable," I point out. The thing looks like it's one second from falling apart. "You could sleep in here. The bed is so big I'd bet we'd never even touch each other. We could even make a pillow line down it. You know, like a border and each of us stays on our side and then everything is perfect."

Why am I still talking? Why can't I ever just shut up?

"I didn't realize pillows could make everything perfect," he answers, but his tone sounds amused. At least, that's better than the annoyance he seems to feel toward me.

I sit up and turn on the bedside lamp again before grabbing pillows. I arrange them in a careful line down the blankets. "See? It's comfortable for both of us now." I risk a glance at him which is a huge mistake. Because the man is wearing gray sweatpants. Gray sweatpants and nothing else. Gray sweatpants that hug a very prominent bulge.

Does this mean he likes me or is that just a normal reaction to something else? Should I say something about it? No, definitely don't want to make this anymore awkward than it already is.

He stalks across the hardwood floor and eases down on the mattress gingerly with his back to me.

It's covered with scars. He's been hurt before, white marks that go up and down his back. I saw something like that once in my history book. It was a picture of a man who had been whipped.

My breath catches in my throat at the thought that someone hurt this big man in the same way.

"I was a troubled kid," he says, seeming to understand my response. "Had it coming."

I can't stop myself from reaching out. My fingertips ghost along the scars, my own heart hurting. Who did this to him? Is this why he understands what it's like to be on the run? He said he had to leave everything behind once too. "No kid deserves this."

"Molly," his voice is strained, angry. "The border exists for a reason."

I snatch my hand back, feeling as if I've been burned. My cheeks sting from the harsh reprimand. I mumble an apology and turn onto my side, blinking back tears. For the things he must have gone through as a kid. For the way I keep being an idiot who puts herself out there.

I feel the mattress dip as he settles onto it. He adjusts his pillow twice before he sighs. "I'm not good with people."

I don't say anything. I'm not sure if he's trying to

apologize or explain. Then again, it doesn't matter. He has every right to be mad at me. Here I am crashing into his life, and he's gone out of his way to be kind, but I keep wanting to cling to him like a barnacle.

"Or being touched," he adds.

My heart breaks even more at his confession. I don't know what to say. It must have taken Trace a lot to be vulnerable with me and I worry I'll get this wrong just like I have everything else with him. In the end, I don't say anything and eventually I drift to sleep and dream of a scowling mountain man with piercing blue eyes.

THE NEXT DAY, I HALF EXPECT TO WAKE TO TRACE sending me away. But he doesn't. Of course, he doesn't. He's too kind, too gracious to send a home-less woman away from his presence. I resolve to do better by him. I'll work harder, study him and learn what makes him happy. Would he let me stay then?

I brush away the question as his phone lights up with a call. I pause where I'm standing in front of the mirror, gurgling mouthwash, to glance at the screen.

Fear shoots through me when I see the call is

from a cancer center. Is he sick? Is that why he's out here all alone? Has he come out here like a wounded animal to prepare himself for the end?

I slip the device into the pocket of my blue jeans. When I woke up this morning, my clothes were freshly laundered and folded, waiting on the bed. Everything was there, even my bra and panties.

Trace and Princess were already gone from bed. She sleeps in the bed with him, curls up on his chest and purrs until she falls into a peaceful slumber. I spent half the night jealous of her and how he kept absently stroking her fur even in his sleep.

The smell of bacon and eggs has me walking to the kitchen in a daze. I have to pass through the living room as I go. It looks better without all the junk. It still needs a serious overhaul, but I can do it. I can make this place cozy and homey for Trace.

Swallowing back tears, I prepare myself to face him. He doesn't strike me as the type that would want anyone to make a big fuss over the fact that he's sick, and I promise myself to face this stoically.

He's at the stove when I come in, frying bacon and humming along to the radio as he works. It's another classical piece, and I wonder if he's always loved this music or if his cat is the reason he enjoys it.

Princess is on the floor, enjoying what I think might be a homemade meal. It shouldn't surprise me that he takes such good care of his cat. Trace might like to pretend otherwise but he has a big heart. A big, beautiful heart.

He looks up from the stove. "You're just in time. Food is done."

I pull the phone from my pocket, feeling like it burns my fingertips. "You, um, you missed a call."

He places the device on the counter without even looking at it. He points with the spatula. "Thanks. Grab plates for me. That cabinet."

I get the plates and hand them to him right as I burst into tears.

7
TRACE

I woke up this morning with one resolution: I will not make Molly sad today. I could tell last night that I hurt her. But I didn't know how to fix it. People aren't something I understand, and that's never bothered me. With Molly though, I find myself wanting to try. I want to understand her and be there for her.

When she comes into the kitchen, her face is pale. She's probably expecting me to pull another Jekyll and Hyde. I won't do that today. "You're just in time. Food is done."

She's back in her clothes this morning which disappoints me even though I'm the one who set them out for her. Part of me had hoped to wake her with breakfast in bed, to cuddle her warm-from-sleep body close. It was a stupid fantasy.

She pulls my phone from her pocket. "You, um, you missed a call."

Something isn't right. I set the phone down on the counter, more concerned with comforting Molly than figuring out who would have called. I point the spatula in the direction of the nearby cabinet. "Thanks. Grab plates for me. That cabinet."

I didn't realize how much I'd like to cook for two until this morning. A man could get used to this. He could wake up every morning to spoil his girl with her favorite breakfast foods. Nope, not mine. Got to keep that in mind.

She passes me the plates, but something is definitely wrong with her expression. Then without warning, she bursts into tears. Not the quiet little tears you can wipe away discreetly. These are big, heaving sobs.

I toss the plates down on the counter and my hands are on her shoulders before I even realize I'm touching her. "You don't have to eat the scrambled eggs."

"It's not that," Molly hiccups. She throws herself into my chest, wrapping her arms around my middle and squeezing me tight. Her tears wet my t-shirt as I rub her back and try to figure out what the hell is going on.

I let her cry, waiting for her storm to pass. The moment she tells me who made her sob like this, that motherfucker is dead. No one makes my beautiful girl cry.

When she finally stops, I step back long enough to reach for a paper towel. I clean the tears from her face and force myself to stay calm until I have the name of the person whose ass will be getting kicked today. "Tell me what's going on."

"You're so strong and brave and really nice." She sniffs. Her eyes are red and puffy, and she looks like she might start crying again any minute now. "And I know you wouldn't want me making a big fuss over you, but you'll just have to deal with that." She pushes her finger into my chest. "Because we're friends and it's OK to be sad when your friend is sick."

I capture her hand and bring it to my lips. I press a soft kiss to her palm, unable to resist. I need to be touching her all the time, the urge only grows every minute I'm around her and I can no longer fight it. I'm tired of holding myself back. "What do you mean sick?"

"I saw the call was from the cancer center."

"That's why you were crying? You were crying for me?" The thought nearly drives me to my knees. No one has ever cried for me. No one has ever cared about my pain. But I've barely known this woman twenty-four hours and she's shown me more compassion than I've ever received in my life.

"You don't have to pretend. I get it. You're a big, bossy mountain man who doesn't need anybody. But it's OK to be scared or sad or whatever it is you feel. This is a big deal, and I'm your friend and I'm here for you."

I blow out a breath. This woman is killing me in the best way. She's too damn sweet, too damn precious. Why the universe delivered her to me, I'll never know. But I'm not letting her go now. I'm all in, and that means telling her things. Having conversations that are going to destroy me. "I don't have cancer."

"Then why—?"

"Eat and I'll tell you what you want to know," I answer, grabbing the plates. I make her a big helping of the now cold food and settle at the table.

She's across from me when we sit and that's not good enough. I need to feel her next to me. I move my chair until I'm by her side, only then feeling peace and contentment. Will she still want me when she knows everything? It doesn't matter because now she's stuck with me. I'm hers.

She clasps her hands together in her lap like she's preparing herself for the worst. "Tell me."

"Take a bite first," I answer. I need to know she's eating, that all of her needs are being met. More than that, I need to know that I'm the one meeting those needs.

She does as I instructed then looks up at me. Her eyes are still bright, but she seems calmer.

I take a deep breath, searching for the words. I've never talked about this with anyone. Never wanted to bare my heart. "The scars on my back are from my stepfather. He's dying of cancer now, and he's looking to make peace with me."

I'm not sure about that last part since I haven't talked to him or my mom. All I have is a garbled voice message from a nurse at the facility. From what I could tell, he's sick with cancer and I guess, some stupid part of me hopes that he is trying to make amends. A bigger part of me suspects the man who tormented me as a boy wants to get a few more blows in.

"What a bastard." She stabs one of the eggs on her plate with far more force than necessary. "He wants peace? He doesn't fuckin' deserve it!"

I chuckle at her language, even though my stomach is tight. "He's not a bad guy. Just tried to raise me the best way he knew how."

She drops her fork and scowls. "You're telling me that if you had a child, you'd let someone do that to them?"

"Fuck no." I'd die before I'd let something happen to any baby of mine. But now the image of having children is in my head and I'm wondering what Molly would look like with her stomach rounded with my kid.

Her gaze softens. "Then don't defend the monster."

I push away my plate, my food untouched. I haven't thought about this stuff in years. I've managed to keep it carefully caged. "He's not the monster. I am."

"You were a child, Trace." So sweet. So trusting. She believes that I'm good. Will an angel like her forgive the beast I am? Will she offer me absolution? At the very least, she won't run screaming. She's too kind for that.

"My real father was a…" Intellectually, I know what he is, but I've never said it out loud. "A serial rapist."

I brace myself for her to leave, to tell me I'm a

disgusting piece of shit. But instead of turning away from me, she grasps my hand. Her delicate fingers with the chipped red nail polish squeeze my big, hairy ones. She's touching me. I marvel at the small miracle.

"It's OK. You can tell me. Tell me about all the broken places," she encourages.

The shame threatens to pull me under, and I fight the urge to drop her hand and disappear into my workshop. "My mom was already married at the time. She had three daughters and her husband feared what I'd become. He thought…the apple doesn't fall far from the tree."

She pushes away from the table, and I wait for her to walk out without a word. But she folds herself into my lap, putting her head on my chest. She's sitting side saddle and staring up at me with such trust. "You're not like that."

I have to swallow a lump in my throat. She barely knows me, yet she trusts me completely, offering me grace. "His theory was that he could beat the devil out of me. He thought if he did, I could grow up to be good."

My voice breaks on the last word but I force myself to keep talking, telling her things that are cutting me open. "I'm the furthest thing from good. I thought I was managing it, then I met you and now I want…*things*…with you."

After my confession, I don't even dare breathe. I just sit with her in my arms, a monster awaiting judgement from this angel.

She doesn't freak out. She's quiet for a long moment before she softly asks, "Like touching each other?"

"And other things." I want her naked, pressing up against me. I want to touch every inch of her skin and have her touch me in return. "That's the kind of fucked up I am."

Her hand slips beneath my t-shirt and she presses her palm over my heart. It's thumping under her touch. "Then I'm just as fucked up because I want *things* with you too."

8

MOLLY

My beautiful, scarred mountain man. How long has he carried this pain? How long has he been made to feel that craving even the slightest human contact was wrong? It's horrible and awful and completely incomprehensible to me.

He stills when I tell him I want things with him too. His breath catches in his throat, his inhale loud in the quiet kitchen.

Suddenly, it makes sense. In the workshop when I thought he was going to kiss me, he didn't. He wanted me and talked himself out of it.

I run my fingers along his beard, feeling his firm jaw underneath it. "You could kiss me now. We could start there. I've heard kissing is nice and—"

My words falter as he surges forward and presses his lips to mine. It's awkward and weird at first, neither of us having much experience. But then he pulls away, frowns, and tries again. This time I'm expecting it and I angle my head to match his. Our lips connect in a tender touch, and I like it. I like the way he's so big and hard everywhere else but he's soft here on his lips.

I experiment with sucking on his full bottom lip, not sure if I'm doing this right. But then he growls. Only he doesn't sound annoyed. He sounds... pleased? Yeah, I'm pretty sure that's what that noise was.

He licks my lip in return, and I gasp at the sensation. He uses my surprise to invade my mouth, his tongue gently exploring and stroking mine.

A shiver runs down my spine. This is why people kiss because it feels so good to be touching each other in such an intimate place.

He only stops kissing me when we're both desperate for air, our breathing loud and harsh.

"Let me try something," I murmur. I twist on his lap, brushing against his hardness. I work to keep my face neutral, so I don't freak him out even though I really want to touch him there. Maybe in time when he knows I'm not going to shame or judge him for the things he needs.

I put my thighs on either side of his and lower myself down slowly. The position opens me up and I release a happy sigh when I feel his bulge against me through our jeans. One day we'll have to do this with nothing between us.

"Fuck, that feels good," he says.

I reach for the hem of my shirt and tug it off, throwing it carelessly onto the floor.

His eyes darken when he takes in the sight of my full breasts in my magenta-colored bra. My nipples tighten in response and there's a pull in my lower belly. Everything in my body is electrified, all my senses sharpened.

He lifts his hand, tracing the swell of my breasts. His touch is soft and reverent, his callouses from years of hard work scraping against my skin. "You're beautiful."

My cheeks heat at his praise. I want him touching me everywhere. "It comes off, my bra, I mean."

It's hard to concentrate when he's looking at me and touching me and making me feel like I am the most beautiful woman in the world.

He hesitates and that's when I remember that he probably doesn't know how to take off a bra. I lean forward, groaning at the soft contact. His bulge is pressing between my thighs and my breasts are against his strong chest. Yeah, we're definitely getting out of these clothes at some point.

"Look on my back. See the clasp?" I tell him. I don't know why I want him to be the one undressing me so badly, but I do.

He experiments with it twice before he gets it.

I sit up and look him in the eyes. I want to watch his expression when he sees my breasts for the first time. "Now tug down the straps."

His fingers shake as he eases them down and drops the bra on the floor. Heat and lust flare in his gaze. For a long second, he doesn't do anything. I'm aching for him to touch them, to feel them.

I let out a breath, reminding myself to relax. But it's hard when I'm wound so tight from wanting him this way. My cheeks heat as I murmur the invitation, "You…maybe, you could touch them."

He takes my breasts in his hands, the ample mounds overflowing. They feel so heavy with him touching them. He runs his thumbs across my puckered peaks, and I groan at the contact.

He glances at me, and I give him an encouraging nod. "Feels really good to have you touching them."

Trace runs his thumb along them again then dips

his head. He presses soft, tender kisses to the valley of my chest before he moves to my breasts.

He continues kissing until he reaches my nipple where he circles it with his tongue. Then he sucks it into his mouth, and I moan so loudly that it should be embarrassing, but this feels so good. Even better than when I imagined it in the bathroom after my shower.

I thread my fingers through his hair, pulling on his silky strands. "Trace, Trace, that's so good."

He rasps his teeth over the sensitive bud, the move making me cry out in pleasure. Why did we waste yesterday cleaning up his place? We could have spent it kissing and touching each other. We could have been doing this in his bed last night.

Trace releases my breast with a wet pop and stares down at it. He blows on my reddened nipple, a smirk lighting up his features when he sees it harden even more. "You like this."

I squirm on his lap, unable to keep still any longer. I rub against his hardness. He's so big everywhere else, it makes me wonder if his cock is big too. Big and thick and powerful, like his fingers. Just the thought is driving me wild. "Touch me in my panties."

He stills and for a moment, I don't think he'll do

it. I worry I've pushed him too far too fast. But after a few seconds, he asks in a strained voice, "Are you sure?"

I whimper and press kisses to the side of his neck. "Please, need you."

"Fuck, fuck," he murmurs and then he's reaching for my blue jeans. He pops the button open easily and shoves his hand into my panties. He groans as he touches my sopping wet center. "You needed this? Needed me touching your pussy?"

"Yes," I cry out, riding his hand with no shame. I need my mountain man. I'll always need him to chase away the ache, to make it better.

I suck the hot skin of his neck into my mouth, running my tongue across him. He tastes salty and musky and male. I can't help but wonder if his cock would taste the same way on my tongue. The thought has me grazing my teeth along the column of his throat at the same moment he shoves one of his big fingers inside of my pussy. He's filling me, owning me, possessing me and nothing has ever felt so right in my life.

Trace uses the pad of his thumb to rub my clit as he continues thrusting his finger into my channel. The room is filled with the wet sounds of his hands on me and his harsh breathing and our frantic heart-beats. I love the filthy soundtrack.

I whimper at the sensation of his fingers touching me in my most intimate area. "Keep… that's…amazing."

I can feel his body tense. The muscles in his thighs tighten and his shoulders are rigid. His jaw is locked so tight that he might just crack a molar as he grinds out, "Come for me."

I'm not sure if it's a plea or a command. It doesn't matter because the moment he says those words I'm tensing around his finger, my orgasm rolling through me. It's fierce and powerful, the storm finally breaking. Pleasure consumes me, and I hump his hand, not caring about anything but chasing that high.

When I finally still, all the tension has drained from my body, and I bury my face in his neck. I never imagined it would feel like that. Sure, I've read a few books about sex but without any female friends, I had no one to talk with. I never expected it to feel so wonderful.

"You did good," Trace murmurs as he pulls his hands from my panties like I was the one making an effort. Still, his words fill me with satisfaction. I think…I want to be his good girl. I want to earn his praise every day.

He rearranges my clothes and it's only then I realize that he didn't get off. "Can I do that for you? I mean, it'd be my first time, but I can give it a try. If you show me what you like—"

He shakes his head, a soft pink tinge coloring his cheeks underneath his beard. "Uh, that's not necessary."

"Oh." Disappointment rolls through me at the thought of not getting to give him the same thing. I try to move from his lap and that's when I realize his jeans are wet too. Really wet and messy and I wasn't the only one who came. Realizing that eases my embarrassment. I can't help grinning. "That was…I liked…can we do it again? Maybe without clothes and—"

He presses a kiss to my lips, a quick peck that silences me. I melt a little more into his hard body as he lets me go.

"Date," he says, and his voice is so deep that he has to clear his throat. "Date first then we'll try again without the clothes."

My heart beats fast at his words. He's taking me on a date. The handsome mountain man wants a date with *me*. I should say something cool and suave. I should show him how grownup I am. "Yuh-huh."

His eyes crinkle in the corners. "How does dinner tonight sound?"

I can't help grinning. I don't care that I probably look like a dork because he likes me. Trace likes me back. "Kind of perfect."

9

MOLLY

I TOWEL DRY MY HAIR AS BEST I CAN. TRACE DOESN'T own a hair dryer or curling iron which means my long hair will have to be braided again. I wish I had what I needed to get dolled up for our date tonight, but somehow, I don't think the giant mountain man will care all that much.

After he asked me out, we spent the day working. We moved two more loads of junk from his home to the workshop. He seemed a little embarrassed that he'd let the place get so bad, but I suppose when you live alone like he does it's hard to care too much.

We didn't touch each other as we worked even when we paused to eat peanut butter sandwiches on the front porch. But we'd do this thing where I'd catch him staring at me and I'd give him a little smile then he would smile too. It felt like we had a big secret from the rest of the world.

I slip into the pretty dress that Cadence, his friend Brennon's wife, dropped off. Apparently, Trace has lots of big, burly mountain friends here and a couple of them are married. She was so sweet and gave me several outfits including pajamas. She even left me her cellphone number.

I acted like I'd misplaced my phone rather than admit I'm on the run. I still haven't figured out what to do about that. I don't think I can stay here in Courage County forever. But the thought of leaving Trace makes me feel hollow inside.

Maybe if my dad's men never find me then it's OK. Maybe if no one ever comes looking for me then I can stay.

Once I've gotten dressed and done the best I can with my hair, I leave the bathroom and give Trace a shy smile. He makes me feel all mushy inside with just a look. "All yours."

"Damn straight," he murmurs. He's sweaty from our earlier work, his t-shirt clinging to him. I wouldn't mind staying in tonight and discovering what his sweaty skin tastes like. But he's being very insistent on the date. The tough welder might try to hide it but he's a gentleman.

"Where are we going for our date?" I ask Trace when we're in his truck. I spent the time he was getting ready, playing with Princess. She's such an affectionate girl. Trace says she's not normally but he's lying. That kitty is pure love.

While he was in the shower, I thought about calling home and trying to contact dad's second in command. My dad wouldn't be missing me, but I could at least figure out how angry he is.

As much as I wanted his affection growing up, he'd never give it to me. I was only a pawn in his eyes and the day I accepted that truth was the day I stepped outside the castle walls.

Now that I've left my tower bedroom, I can't imagine going back. There's too much freedom here and while sometimes it feels scary, I have Trace beside me. I know instinctively that he'll protect me.

"We'll have dinner then I'll show you around town. Afraid we don't have too much in the way of entertainment."

I don't ever want him to feel he has to apologize to me. Any time spent with Trace is a good time. "I'd really like that."

For dinner, Trace takes me to Liquid Courage. It's a bar turned restaurant that's run by Ledger and Peyton Kringle. Yeah, the town has a real live

Christmas tree ranch. There are even tours put on during the holidays.

"We'll go in December," Trace promises after Peyton takes my order back to the kitchen. "I'll get you the biggest Christmas tree we can find."

My stomach flips at his words. He's talking about well over six months from now. He's talking like we'll still be together. What would Christmas with Trace be like? Would we build snowmen together and make snow angels and have snowball fights? Could we snuggle in front of the fire and watch holiday movies?

Tears prick my eyes at the thought of spending those moments with him. After my mom died, Christmas and other holidays lost their meaning. My dad didn't care about celebrating them and it wasn't like I had any friends. Instead, each day passed just like the one before it. There were no celebrations, no birthdays, no way of marking the passing of time with special moments. "It'd be fun to do that."

A few beats of silence pass between us and I wonder if he's thinking about holidays too. Somehow, I imagine that his have been just as sad and lonely as mine. But I don't want either of us thinking about our pasts right now. I want to focus on the present and the beautiful thing we're discovering between us. "How did you get into welding?"

"I left home when I was sixteen. Lived on the streets for a while before Roman found me. He hired me on one of his construction crews. I got to know a few of the guys that did welding. Got into it from there. Eventually, I started creating pieces and they sold well. Enough that I didn't have to be part of a construction crew anymore." He blows out a breath, looking surprised that he's talked so much about himself. "What about you? Where do you come from?"

I can't answer that question. There's a lot I can't tell him about my past. Not if I want to keep him safe. The thought fills me with sadness because I want to let Trace in. I want him to know everything about me. Instead, I shrug. "Here and there."

Disappointment flickers across his face, but he nods. "How about clay? You said you're an artist. How did you get to working with that medium?"

I think of how I can answer those questions without revealing too much. But before I can respond, Peyton arrives with our dinner of fish and chips. The food is perfectly crispy and greasy, and Trace lets me steal fries from his plate after I finish mine.

As long as I'm careful, I can give him some pieces of my story. "I've always liked art, and I've tried a lot of different things. Watercolor painting and drawing with charcoal and even some woodworking. Nearly sliced off a finger." I hold out my hand to show him the faint scar along my pinkie. "After that, my dad said no more woodworking. It was probably for the best. I wasn't very good at it."

He chuckles and thankfully doesn't touch on the topic of my father. "So, after that you started with clay?"

I nod and push away my now empty plate. "I'm making complex things now—entire villages and little scenes. I'd like to make a dollhouse. Make all the furniture. I think that would be fun. Maybe in time I could do something, like turn it into a career. But I don't know what. Actually, it sounds kind of dumb when I say it out loud." I chew on my lower lip. My dad would have laughed at my dreams. He would have told me I'm stupid.

But Trace brightens at my words. He glances at the clock on his phone then pushes to his feet. "Come on, I want to show you something."

We walk down Main Street together and when Trace links his fingers through mine, I think I could float away. I glance at our hands. Then I look up and he's looking at me again and we both smile at the same time. A bubbly, giggly feeling fills me. I don't know what it is exactly, but I like it.

He leads me into a little shop with a sign over it that reads *Seize the Clay*. A woman with red ringlets peeks out behind shelves of clay creations. There's a collection of gnomes on one shelf, and another shelf features puppies chasing each other through long, tall grass. There's so much to see and my fingers itch to reach out and touch them all. "Welcome to—oh, hey, Trace. Who's your friend?"

He introduces me to Summer, the owner of the shop, then adds, "She makes things with clay too."

My cheeks heat. "N-not like you. Your stuff is really cool."

Her eyes light up and she links her arm through mine before taking me around the shop to discuss her various creations. She asks me lots of questions about what I do and even shows me the classroom where she teaches other people how to get started in clay.

"You've built a whole business around this," I say when she's done.

This is what Trace was trying to show me. I could actually take my dream and do something with it. My heart warms at the realization and I glance across the shop to where he's standing.

He's near the front door, talking with another man that Summer introduced earlier as her husband, Cash. Apparently, the two of them were friends for a long time before they decided to make a baby together.

I watch Trace grunt out answers as Cash tries to engage him in conversation. I don't think my mountain man cares much for small talk but he's making an effort to be here for me.

I remember the way he bought me. He didn't even know me and yet he didn't hesitate to step in and rescue me. He's fed me and clothed me. He's even fingered me to an incredible orgasm.

That bubbly, giggly feeling floats through me again and I think that maybe I'm falling in love with the handsome mountain man.

Just as the realization comes, movement in the corner behind Trace catches my eye, and I stiffen. Was that one of my father's men? Have they found me already?

10

TRACE

MOLLY IS DIFFERENT AFTER HER VISIT TO SUMMER'S shop. At first, I thought she was just taking it all in. But the further we get up the mountain, the more it seems a blanket of sadness is wrapping around her.

I don't know what to say, how to reach her. I want to help her, to let her know that her troubles aren't just hers anymore.

When I tried to get the most basic information from her on our date, she wouldn't answer the question. Part of me wants to grab her and demand she trust me. The part of me that's spent time on the streets and seen so much cruelty knows that trust has to be earned.

Still, it bothered me the way she kept looking

over her shoulder on our date. She didn't have to be scared. I was already on alert, and I have the sheriff looking out for her. He'll let me know if anyone new comes through town.

Back at my cabin, I start to go inside but she lingers on the front porch. She leans across one of the railings, staring up at the night sky. "You go ahead. I'm going to watch the stars for a little while."

Something in me tingles, an awareness that I shouldn't leave her alone right now. "Then we'll watch the stars together. I know the perfect place."

I grab a blanket from the back of my truck before I lead her deeper into my property. I love living in these woods. I love having them all to myself and knowing I'm the only one around for miles.

In the fading light of dusk, she follows after me, pausing at one point to grip the back of my t-shirt after she nearly trips on a tree branch. I turn and pick her up. Just pull her into my arms and carry her because it feels natural and right. Like I should be doing this all the time.

She nestles into my chest, and it occurs to me that she never fights me or protests being carried. She just cuddles deeper into my embrace, and it makes me worry that maybe she's never been loved well. Maybe she's like me, a lonely survivor craving the warmth of another person.

Her voice is muffled by my shirt. "Trace, if I stayed with you forever, would you carry me like this again?"

I tighten my hold on her at the thought of forever. I've never wanted that with anyone but with her, I do. I want Molly to be my forever. "Always."

She lets out a little sigh of contentment. "That's what I thought."

I put her down only long enough to spread out the blanket underneath the shade of my favorite oak tree. The ground is still wet from last night's rain and the branches form a canopy above, letting us stare up at the night sky.

As soon as we're settled, I pull her back into my arms. She's between my legs, her back against my chest. My hip is throbbing, but I ignore the pain. It's worth it when I can feel each inhale of breath as she takes it and her thick hips between my hands. This is what heaven feels like.

"This is a pretty tree." She isn't aware of the way she keeps running her fingers up my thigh then down to my knee and back again. She isn't aware of what it's doing to me or how badly I need to grind against her hot little body.

I don't want to come right here just from her simple touch. I already embarrassed myself once today when I came in my jeans at the table. I fought it for as long as I could. But having her wriggling all over my lap and squeezing my fingers so tight in that warm pussy of hers made me shoot my load too fast. Here I am likely to do it again. "This is a Northern Red Oak, part of the Beech family. To be specific, it's the Fagaceae species."

"That's…interesting," she manages. Her tone indicates that she's not fascinated by my little facts at all. But it doesn't matter because trees are a safe subject. Trees don't make me think about spreading her out on this blanket and railing into her over and over again until she screams my name at the heavens.

"There are over four hundred types of flowering plants, trees, and shrubs within it. Many of them deciduous, meaning—"

She angles her head up and presses a soft kiss to my lips, interrupting my botany presentation right in the middle. "You're making it hard for a girl to seduce you."

My brain is still scrambled from that kiss, and it takes a moment for her words to finally penetrate the haze. When it does, I blurt out what I've been thinking about all day, "I want to taste your pussy."

She groans. "I like it when you say dirty things."

I move my hands up and gently touch the sides of her breasts. She showered tonight before our date and I spent the time on my phone, looking up every article I could on how to eat pussy. Maybe it should embarrass me that I've never been with another woman, but it doesn't. I love the thought that I'm just hers. That no one else will ever know my body the way she will.

She arches into my touch. "Can you say other dirty things?"

I didn't think to look up anything dirty to say, but it doesn't matter. I wouldn't have wanted to use anyone else's lines. I'd rather just be honest with her, tell her what I'm really thinking. "While we were working, I kept thinking about bending you over and shoving my cock into your juicy cunt."

She chuckles. "Really?"

I move my hands to the front of her breasts, pinching her nipples through her clothes. "I thought about how your tits bounced when you were on my lap today. How I want to see that again."

I press soft kisses to the side of her neck. She's so soft everywhere and her skin tastes like sugar. Fuck,

I could get drunk off of her sweet taste. She already has me addicted, desperate to feel and taste and suck on every inch of her.

Reaching for her dress, I fumble with the top buttons. There are too many of them and they're keeping me from seeing my girl's gorgeous tits again. "Get this dress off."

She whimpers at my words but pushes to her feet. She shimmies out of the material until she's only left in her bra and panties in the moonlight. She turns to me, her eyes searching mine.

"I've never seen a sight prettier," I quickly reassure her, pushing to my feet too. I'll spend every day of the rest of my life telling my girl how beautiful she is. I don't want her to ever doubt it for even a moment.

I pull the band holding her hair in a braid and finger comb it loose. There's something about seeing her long hair between my thick fingers that makes me smile. She's small and delicate yet she trusts me. She trusts me to care for her.

I take her bra and panties next. I go as slow as I can, just to tease her. Just to make her ache the way she's kept me aching all day. The smell of her arousal hits me in the gut and has my mouth watering.

"Now lie down on the blanket," I instruct.

She does as I asked, peering up at me again.

I drop to my knees, biting back a curse at the pain. "You're such a good girl."

When I said it and she was on my lap, her eyes dilated, and her breathing hitched. The two responses told me she likes it when I praise her. "You're my good girl and I'm going to reward you. I'm going to put my face between your thighs and make you scream."

An owl hoots, the wind whistles through the tree branches and in the distance, an animal roams through the woods. Nothing else matters though except that I'm here with my woman under the light of a full moon.

I press gentle kisses to her tummy going lower and lower until I'm at her mound. She's beautiful, a full proud bush that makes me even harder. Her curly hairs are already damp from her arousal.

I spread her pussy lips and lick her slit. Her flavor explodes on my tongue, sweet and satisfying. Exactly what I've been craving today.

She moans when I do it again, a soft breathy sound that fills me with contentment. I want to spend the rest of my life learning her different moans and memorizing all of them. I want her always on her back, pretty thighs spread for me as she shows me her wet pussy. Guess it's my pussy now. Because I own this woman, and no one is taking her from me.

I continue to stroke her with my tongue, mapping her body, until she's yanking on my hair and murmuring incoherently. That's when I move higher, going for her clit. The little nub is already swollen and puffy. I suck it into my mouth at the same time I ease a finger into her tight channel. Her thighs clamp around my ears and she raises her hips, offering herself to me.

I keep playing with that little nub and working another finger into her. I'm sucking and teasing until she's bucking and yelling my name into the night. Fuck the suburbs. We're never living there. We'll always be out here in the country where she can scream her pleasure out to the universe.

I continue stroking her body as she floats back down. Then I yank off my clothes and toss them. I'll never find them again in the dark. But then again, that might give me the perfect excuse to keep her here until dawn. The thought of spending the night making love to her curvy body has more precum leaking from my cock.

I strangle the fucker, willing him to behave. That's for her now. All of me is for her, but especially my come. The only place I want that is between her pretty thighs where it belongs.

Stretching out above her, I support my weight on my forearms. My cock nestles next to her hot pussy, and I breathe a sigh of relief. Being on top of her with all of our naked skin touching makes me feel like I've found home.

I kiss her again and when our lips connect, she groans at her own flavor. As far as I'm concerned, her essence is my new favorite one. I'll always want her taste on my tongue.

"You're going to take my cock now," I tell her. "But I'll make this good for you. I'll get you addicted. You'll crave my cock day and night. Now spread those pretty thighs wide for me. As wide as you can. Your man is big. There's a good girl."

I notch my head at her entrance before glancing up. I want to see her face, memorize the first moment she sees me move inside of her. I mean to go slow but her pussy sucks me in deep and before I know it, I'm pushing all the way inside.

She lets out her breath. "You're so thick. So hard. Does it always feel this good?"

I pull out only to ram back into her, my heavy

balls slapping against her ass. Damn, I don't think it gets better than this. Better than being connected to my woman in every way. "It's good because it's you and me."

When I slip out of her this time, I reach for her clit, circling it around the way I did earlier with my tongue. Sweat coats my body and the scent of our arousal mixes with the earthy smells of dirt and dew. "Give me one more."

"I don't think—" She protests as her nails scrabble for purchase on my arms. She's raising her hips up, bucking against me and seeking her next release.

"I said one more," I grunt and pinch her clit.

She detonates on the spot, clawing at me and howling my name to the heavens. I join her chorus of noises, coming with a roar of my own.

It's only as my hot seed fills her that I realize I didn't ask her about birth control. Probably because knowing she was on anything that would keep my sperm from getting to her eggs would anger me. I want this woman pregnant with my babies.

She moans my name one last time when we've both stilled. For a moment, I don't move. I don't do anything but close my eyes and focus on the weird sensation in my chest. It takes me a moment to understand what it is. Love. I'm in love with this woman.

I glance down at her and see her eyelids getting heavy. I press a soft kiss to her forehead. Tomorrow we'll talk. Tonight, I'll get her back in my bed where she belongs.

I carry her home using the light of the forest to guide me. When I place her in our bed, a wave of satisfaction goes through my body. "Sleep, sweet girl. I'll wear you out again tomorrow."

"Tomorrow," she whispers and snuggles against my body.

I close my eyes and drift into a dreamless sleep that's only interrupted when I hear the soft noise of Princess meowing.

I reach to put my hand on her, to comfort her in my half-awakened state. But she's not on my chest like she normally is. No, she's somewhere else.

Forcing my eyes open, I glance around the room. Not only is Princess not in the bed, neither is Molly. She's not anywhere.

That's when I hear Princess meow again. It's a mournful sound, as if she's grieving something.

Molly's musical voice is next. "Listen, I know you're sad that I'm leaving. I am too. But you have to take good care of your daddy for me. He's a really special man."

This woman thinks she can leave me? Hell no. I'm not letting that happen. Not tonight or any other night. She belongs to me, and it's time she learns that.

11

MOLLY

It's only when Trace is snoring that I finally leave the bed. The moment I do, I feel so cold, and it has nothing to do with the fact that I'm still naked.

I search the laundry hamper in the bathroom until I finally find my clothes. I slip into the jeans and t-shirt again.

I arrived here with only the clothes on my back, and I won't take anything of Trace's as I leave. He's already been so kind to me, and after everything we shared tonight, I know I'm in love with him. He's wrecked me in the best way.

But my father will come for me. Maybe not today or tomorrow but soon and I know Trace. He won't let me go without a fight. This mountain man would die for me, and that's not a risk my heart can take.

I'd rather live on the run with these beautiful memories than to watch Trace be gunned down. A world where he doesn't exist is too horrible for me to contemplate. My heart can survive anything if my man is alive.

When I'm done, I move to the living room and survey the place. It's already looking so much cleaner and brighter since I arrived. It still needs some pretty throw pillows and maybe a cheerful rug. But it won't be me that gets to decorate his cabin. Some other woman will do that someday.

Princess meows and I look down to see her staring at me. I didn't even hear her leave the bed. She must have followed me out here.

"I know, girl," I whisper and wipe tears from my cheeks. I turn for the door but when she meows again, it's such a pitiful sound that I face her. Bending down, I take a seat on the floor and stroke her soft fur. "Listen, I know you're sad that I'm leaving. I am too. But you have to take good care of your daddy for me. He's a really special man."

"And he's mad as hell that his girls aren't where they belong. In his bed," Trace answers, his voice booming.

I raise my gaze to see him standing there in the doorway of the living room. He's thrown on another

pair of gray sweatpants, but he didn't bother with a
shirt, showing off his hairy chest that I still want to
lick my way down. Fire burns in his eyes. "You think
you're leaving me?"

I swallow down everything I feel for this man, all
the love and the lust and the longing. "Trace, this
was never supposed to be permanent."

"Well, it is now."

"You don't understand," I try to explain as the
tears start again. "He's coming for me. I'm not free to
be with you."

He crosses his arms over his broad chest. When
he does, I see the scratches from where my nails dug
into his flesh only hours ago as he pounded into me,
delivering the most delicious orgasm. "Who? Who's
coming for you?"

I shake my head and reach for the door. It's easier
to just go than stand here and explain. Once he
knows, he'll want me gone anyway. Trace loves his
peaceful existence here on his mountain and when
my world crashes into his, everything will change
for him.

He moves so quickly that I don't even see him.
He's just there one second later with his hand
against the door, blocking my exit. "You don't get

how this works. I love you and that means I won't let you go. You're mine now."

I blink, trying to clear away the tears that are blurring my vision. "You love me?"

"I love you," he repeats. "I love the way you babble when you're nervous and how you sing in the shower and the way you bite your lip when you're trying to concentrate on a hard task."

"We barely know each other," I answer, shaking my head. You can't love someone this quickly. We can't really be in love with each other. Not for real. This is just some fairytale we've convinced ourselves we're living in.

He takes my hand and presses it over his heart. "Feel this? It beats for you now. Just you. I know you're scared, but your heart and mine—they recognized each other. It's why we're so good together."

His heart beats steady and strong underneath my fingertips. This man means everything to me. But can we really win against my dad?

"I'm scared," I admit softly.

He gathers me in his arms and carries me back to his bed with Princess trailing after us. "It's OK to be scared, sweet girl. You lay that fear on me. You put all your burdens on me now. Don't carry it alone anymore."

I settle on the bed and decide to start with the truth of who I am. "My dad is…he's Marco Rossi."

Recognition flickers across his face. My dad isn't the most well-known mob boss in New York, but people still know his name. He has a reputation for being old-school. He believes in making money and keeping a low profile, not drawing attention to his dirty business dealings. "And you're running from him."

I nod and pick at one of the blankets on his bed, plucking at a loose string. "He promised me in marriage to Luis Bianchi."

Trace growls when I tell him that.

His possessiveness makes me smile despite what we're talking about. "He's…not a nice guy. His first two wives have disappeared under mysterious circumstances, but the police can't touch him."

Everyone knows that Luis has a hand in his wives' death. It's no great secret, but the fact that nothing can be proved has kept him out of jail so far. Sometimes, innocent until proven guilty only makes the monsters bolder.

"I ran about a month before my wedding. The guards at my house have a weekly poker night, and I spiked their drinks. It wasn't hard. Just used some of my dad's old sleeping pills."

"Fuck," he breathes softly.

"The Bianchi Family won't forgive the insult which means my dad will come for me," I explain as I nibble on my thumbnail. "I fucked up. I fucked up big time, Trace. I don't see a way out of this, and I don't…I can't stand the idea that you might be hurt."

He wraps his arm around my shoulders. "I'll fix this."

I bark out a laugh. "Yeah, because the mob is known to be so forgiving."

"Do you trust me?" He growls the words out.

I think of the way he handled the men that were selling him the car. He displayed no fear and sent them away. "I trust that you'll do whatever it takes. I trust that you'll always have my back. I don't trust that you're bulletproof. That's what scares me." I whisper the last part, "I can't lose you. You're my other half."

"You won't lose me. The difference between me and your father is he's fighting for power, greed, and dominance. I'm fighting for the woman I love, and love is the strongest force on earth."

I let out a slow breath. I hope he's right. If he's wrong, then we're both going to die because I can't live without him.

12

TRACE

"What do you think?" I ask as I push the new couch into position in the living room. It's been a week since that night I explained to Molly she's mine. She hasn't tried to leave again since.

She surveys the gray couch with her hands on her hips and her lips pursed. We finished removing all the scrap metal and now she's focused on turning my little cabin into a home. She's anxious a lot so I keep her busy and when that doesn't work, well, orgasms are a hell of a relaxant.

In the meantime, I have Roman pulling up everything he can on the Rossi and Bianchi families. Bianchi went mysteriously missing three days ago. His number two is suspected of being behind that, but it's not like anyone cares. The guy was hardly a saint. That just leaves Marco Rossi for me to deal with.

"I think we need some really cool artwork above it." She beams up at me. "What if we check your shop? I bet you have something that would fit perfectly!"

It's on the tip of my tongue to tell her it seems pretentious to display my own work, but the look she gives me is filled with so much happiness that I find myself grabbing my keys and my phone.

She wants to learn to drive. Apparently, her father never let her drive or have a bank account or anything that might possibly lead her to become independent. The fact that he treated her like an object to be kept on a shelf until the time was right fills me with rage. She's so smart and so curious about the world around her.

I wanted to add her name to my bank account and my property deed. But she talked me out of doing it. She pointed out that it would attract her father's attention too early. She's right but it burns in me that she's still being controlled by that asshole.

When we're at the workshop, she spends her time looking through my collection. She carefully fingers each one, running her fingers over the metal as though they're precious to her. Finally, she selects one. It's a silhouette of a cat on a throne, a nod to Princess. She holds it up triumphantly. "This is it!"

I smile at her enthusiasm. Her smile doesn't quite reach her eyes these days but she's trying.

My phone rings and I silence the call. It's the third time in the last two days that someone from the cancer center has reached out. I never listen to the messages or return the calls. I have more important things to do, like love my woman's curvy body.

She frowns at it. "I hate that man. I hope he goes to hell."

I chuckle. She's made no secret of the fact that she thinks my stepdad was a monster.

She blows out her breath. "Still, I've been thinking. He doesn't deserve peace for what he did. I'll never think that. But you do, so if you have something you need to get off your chest, you should go to him. It might be your last chance to get it out before he's gone."

"I'll think about it." I'm not sure what I would say to the man who tormented me. I'm not sure that there is anything to say. But I admit to being curious. If he passes, what does that mean for me and my mom? She's never searched for me as far as I know. But was that because of him? What about my sisters? Do they want to see me?

THREE DAYS LATER, I FIND MYSELF STARING UP AT THE cancer center in Knoxville. It's a non-descript office building in a good part of town.

I left my warm bed with my sleeping woman to drive here, and I'm not even sure why I did it. Maybe I just need to see if the bastard really is dying.

With a deep breath, I propel myself forward. No point in dragging this out. If I hurry, I'll be back on the road within an hour or two.

Inside the lobby, I give my name and I'm directed through a set of double doors into the patient area. I find his room number easily enough and knock before entering.

My gaze is drawn to the frail man lying in the hospital bed. This man can't be my stepdad. He was ten feet tall with a head full of hair and a body like a truck. But the person lying here has wispy gray hair and he's skeletal, much too tiny to be the monster who tormented me. For a moment, I think I walked into the wrong room.

Then my gaze shifts and I spot my mom in the chair by the side of the bed. Of course, she's beside him. She never once stood up for me. That didn't strike me as odd when I was growing up. But now that I'm with Molly and thinking about having babies of our own, I can't imagine it. I'll always stand up for my kids.

I know the moment my mom spots me, the way her spine stiffens.

I look like him. It's something I hate, something I despise about myself. I have his eyes and his nose, the man from her worst nightmares.

"What's wrong with him?" I ask, my voice hoarse. He's sleeping peacefully. How many nights did he sleep peacefully after beating me? Did he really think he was doing right by me, by my mom?

Sarah, my sister, sniffs. It's only then that I register she's in the room. She's been through four husbands now and has at least five kids by my last count. "He's dying of spinal cancer. He's in constant pain."

It's sick that it gives me a sense of satisfaction to know he's hurting. Maybe if he even feels an ounce of the pain that I felt then he finally realizes what he did.

"What did he want to see me about?" I move from the doorway into the room, standing by the bed. It's not lost on me that he's the vulnerable one now. He's the one who's small and has something to fear.

"I'm the one who called," my mom snaps. It's the first time she's spoken to me since I arrived.

I keep my gaze on my stepdad's sleeping form. I wonder if he can hear my voice. Does mine haunt his nightmares the same way his voice has haunted me?

"He's being transferred to hospice care later," she explains.

I still wait, barely breathing. Everything in me is screaming at me to turn around and run. There's a little boy inside that just wants to close his eyes and pretend this isn't happening.

She continues, "I want him home with me. He should be by family when he dies."

I shrug, still not sure where I fit into all of this. "Then take him back home."

Sarah huffs like I'm being intentionally dense. "He'd need round-the-clock nurses. They're expensive."

A wave of cold washes over me, just like it used to when the beatings got bad. I'm no longer here. No longer inside of myself. Instead, I'm outside of my body, watching the scene unfold.

"You could offer to help," Mom suggests. She knows I'm wealthy now. I keep a low profile but word gets out eventually. "He fed you and clothed you all those years. Kept a roof over your head."

"And beat me. You forgot that part," I add. Except I don't feel angry. I don't feel anything. I haven't been this numb in years and even though some part of me knows it's not good, I don't care.

"He was only helping you," she snaps as if I'm an ungrateful child. "He didn't have to keep you. I wanted you gone but he swore to me he could raise you to be good."

I shouldn't have expected her to be sorry. I shouldn't have expected them to care at all. I embrace the numbness, calling on it to get me through these next few moments. "I'll sign the paperwork today. But in return, you never contact me again. No one does. Not when he dies, not when you die, not for funerals or births or baptisms. Nothing. I'm dead to all of you after this."

Mom nods quickly and it dawns on me that she's glad. She's just as glad to be done with me as I am with her. The thought should hurt but it doesn't.

Instead, I follow her to the back and sign a lot of paperwork. I'm not even sure what I'm signing or how expensive this will run. I don't care about the money. It's a small price to pay to finally be rid of the family that never wanted me.

When I'm done, I step into the cancer center parking lot. The sun is shining down on my back, but I can't feel it. I still can't feel anything.

In the distance, I hear my name. Someone is shouting my name.

I look around to see a blur of blonde hair running toward me. Molly is calling my name then throwing herself into my arms. I stagger back under the unexpected weight as she peppers my face with kisses. She came to find me.

My sunshine wraps her arms around my neck and whispers into my ear, "I didn't want you to be alone."

13

MOLLY

"Are you ready to go?" Blade grunts at me as I slide into his truck. He's not happy about this little impromptu road trip.

Trace left earlier this morning while I was still sleeping. When I woke up, there was a knowing deep in my gut.

Blade was on the front porch, drinking a coffee and watching the sunrise. He'd been stationed there. Actually, a lot of his friends were stationed around the property. Because Trace left me protected. He left me in the hands of the best men he knows.

Still, I can't let him be alone in this. There's so much hurt that he's faced on his own for too long, so I have to see him. I have to get to my man.

"Ready," I answer as I buckle my seatbelt. The

cancer center in Knoxville is only a few hours away from Courage County, which means we should make it by lunch time.

The ride is quiet, passing in a quick blur of mile markers and interstate connections. When we finally pull into the parking lot for the cancer center, I breathe a sigh of relief. I'm here.

I'm out of the truck before Blade even fully stops it, and I spot Trace the moment I'm outside. Then I'm running toward him, shouting his name, and throwing myself into his arms. He stumbles back a half-step before holding his ground.

I press kisses all over his face, relief filling me now that I'm finally with him again. "I didn't want you to be alone."

He holds me tight for a long moment before he puts me down gently. There's a distant look in his eyes and I imagine that facing this today took him back to a dark place.

Two hours later, Trace and I haven't said anything. He's quiet and withdrawn, wrapped up in a world of pain.

I think of a little boy who was made to feel helpless and scared and hated every day for years. My heart aches at the thought, but he's no longer that boy. He's a man now. A strong, confident, rugged mountain man. I need to remind him of that.

When I see the sign for the suit store, I have an idea of how to do it. Blade and I passed this sign on our trip to the center. He's on his way back to Courage in his own vehicle. I haven't seen him for miles.

"Get off at this exit," I tell Trace, finally breaking the quiet.

He doesn't ask me why. He just does it.

I direct him to the suit store, and he frowns. "You want to go shopping now?"

It's the first time he's spoken to me all day. I take his hand and tug him out of the truck and into the store. It's nearly empty, which isn't surprising considering that it's early in the afternoon on a weekday.

I wave away the store employee who offers to help us and pull several dress shirts from the display along with two suit coats and a few ties. I shove the items at him. "Carry these."

I sashay to the dressing room desk and give the bored middle-aged woman my sweetest smile. "He's been working out and I'm not sure of his size anymore. Do you think he could try these on?"

I follow Trace into the dressing room with the plush carpeting and bright lights, locking the door behind us. The upscale place has one of those nice settees in the corner, which is perfect for us.

I direct him to sit and take the clothes, tossing them onto the floor. Then I sink down onto the carpet between his knees. Like this, we're face to face. "You've rescued me and protected me. Every day, you show me how love is supposed to be. You're not just my hero. You're my warrior."

I press my lips to his in a searing kiss. When he responds hungrily, dipping his tongue into my mouth and angling my head, I know I haven't misread things. This is exactly what he needs. I break the kiss and we're both fighting hard to control our breathing, so the saleslady doesn't know what's happening in here.

I lean close to his ear, "Now, fuck your girl-friend's mouth."

"Molly..." he calls my name in a quiet groan but I'm already reaching for his pants. I unbutton them and pull down his zipper before I free his monster cock. It's huge and won't be easy to take. As it is, we have to work him into my tight little pussy every time we have sex.

But I want to give him this. I want to remind him that he's a man. More than that, he's *my* man and I spoil my king.

"Shh," I put my finger to his lips and stroke his cock with my other hand, moving it up and down in a slow rhythm. I don't normally get to touch him. He's too intent on getting inside me. "Your queen is on her knees for you."

I spread a drop of precum around his shaft, keeping my movements slow and measured, building this for him.

His head falls back against the dressing room wall, his body relaxing under my touch. For the first time, I realize I hold just as much power over him as he does me. It's an intoxicating rush.

Dipping my head, I press kisses to the inside of his thighs. I'm here on my knees not just to give him pleasure but to make him feel loved. To show him I adore his body just as much as he does mine.

When I get to his cock, I press a kiss to the tip too, a little bit of his precum leaking onto my lips. I lick the flavor. He's as salty as I imagined, and the thought has my panties getting damp.

"Use me," I whisper before I open my mouth and

take his shaft inside. I only manage an inch or two at first, getting used to the weight on my tongue and the feel against my jaw. He swells even more inside my mouth.

He moans, a low guttural sound. Then he takes my face in his hands and pushes his cock deeper into my mouth before withdrawing. He does it twice more, murmuring, "This time, relax. Take me all the way."

I take a breath, letting him slide to the back of my throat. I gag around him, tears streaming from my eyes as he thrusts.

He pulls back and I take a hurried breath before he's in me again, going so deep. I relax a little more each time, leaning into his rhythm and feeling an ache deep between my thighs.

"So close," he whispers, trying to pull away.

I grip his thighs and refuse to move. I want all of him. I want every drop of his seed, want to feel his cock pulse in my mouth as he comes.

He swears under his breath and then he's coming down my throat. I swallow him, drinking down his essence as he collapses against the wall, spent.

I swirl my tongue around his cock one last time, licking him clean before I tuck him back into his pants. My jaw aches and my lips feel puffy. But it's worth it all for the sated smile he gives me.

He reaches for me, but I shake my head and gather the clothes from the floor. This wasn't about that. This was about giving my man what he needed.

When we walk out of the store, he takes my hand. He still isn't talking but that doesn't bother me. I can feel the lightness in his spirit, and the knowledge that he's finding his way back from that dark place is enough for now.

In the truck, he doesn't start the engine immediately. Instead, he pulls me into his embrace and wraps his arms around me. He holds me for long minutes, pausing every so often to press kisses to my temple or my neck.

The stillness between us is broken only by the ringing of his phone. He answers Roman's call and listens for a moment. "Yeah, gather up the men. Tell them I want to see them first thing tomorrow morning."

I frown at him when he ends it. I'm pretty sure I heard Roman say something about my dad, but his voice was pitched too low for me to make it out. "What's happening?"

"Your father has agreed to meet with me," he answers.

At my worried glance, he says, "You don't have to be afraid. I'll make sure you're far away from it. He won't get anywhere near you."

I shake my head. "No, I want to be there. I need to, Trace. I need to see him again."

He's quiet for so long that at first, I think he's going to overrule me. Then he seems to come to a conclusion and nods. "It won't make a difference anyway. He's not getting you back."

14

MOLLY

"YOU DON'T HAVE TO BE THERE TODAY," TRACE TELLS
me, his gaze meeting mine in the bathroom mirror
as I braid my long hair again. This morning, we're
meeting my dad. He's coming here to Trace's cabin.

He told me last night about signing the paperwork to help his stepdad get the hospice nurses he
needed. Trace sounded so broken as he talked about
it, like he'd betrayed the child he once was. But I just
put my head on his chest and told him that I love his
big, compassionate heart.

"I want to. It's better this way," I answer as I
finish twining the last strands of my hair and secure
it with a tie. Trace faced his past, and I can feel the
change in him. He's different now. The pain hasn't

stopped but he is at peace. He's accepted that he was a child, and he didn't deserve to be abused. Maybe this is how I find my peace too.

He wraps his arms around me, hugging me from behind. "Then let's go deal with this so I can come back and make us pancakes for breakfast."

Trace is a great cook and the idea of spending the morning with him in the kitchen instantly lifts my spirits. He's still not as talkative as I am. I doubt he ever will be, but he listens to everything I say and lets me chat for hours on end.

When we step outside, we're not alone. Roman is on the porch waiting for us. He greets Trace with a thump on the back but only nods to me.

"Everyone in place?" Trace asks just as a dark SUV pulls up on the property. Three men dressed in black exit it and wait on the grass. The sight makes my stomach churn. This is it. This is really happening.

"Everyone in place," Roman answers casually, like they're discussing the weather and not the fact that the freakin' mafia is here.

My legs tremble and my knees feel like they might give out, but I still move to the front yard. I walk beside Trace, careful to stay next to him. He's my shield. He always will be. He's the only reason I have the courage to face my father like this.

Carl opens the back door of the SUV and Marco Rossi steps down. He has that cold, calculating look in his eyes and for the first time in my life, I realize it's like seeing a stranger. Back before mom died, he was a different person. A caring and involved father, someone who loved me. Now there's nothing left of his soul, and it shows on his face.

"I see you've found my daughter," Marco nods to Trace as though I were a lost child and not a grown adult who ran from a forced marriage. "What would you like for her return?"

Trace grunts. His whole body is tensed as he evaluates my father.

"I'm not going back, dad," I tell him quietly. Calling him dad feels weird. I can't remember the last time I actually called him that.

But my dad just smiles. To him, this is another business deal and there's nothing my father enjoys more than negotiations. He continues to talk with Trace, "Money? I have plenty of it. Connections? I have them all over the globe. Fame? I can grant you that too."

Roman snorts, clearly not impressed with the offers.

"I said no," I repeat, my voice firmer this time.

My dad finally glances from Trace to me. "I suppose you think you're in love with him. Maybe even spread your legs for him, you whore."

My cheeks flame, and shame fills me. Is that what he thinks of me? Does he think Trace is only with me because I've slept with him?

"Watch the way you speak to my future wife," Trace growls, his fingers curling into fists. My dad probably has men crawling all over this property, deep in the forest. But I'd still bet that Trace could take on his whole army.

"She's not your property," my father repeats.

Trace shakes his head, a smile playing at his lips. His hand finds mine and he gives it a gentle squeeze. "Some addicts coming through here sold her to me, so yeah, she is mine."

My father waves a hand. "I understand. You're a businessman. You're looking for a return on your investment, so name your price."

Roman coughs, and Trace doesn't even spare him a glance. I think it may have been some signal between the two of them. But I'm too busy watching my dad and Carl, his second-in-command. I'm worried they'll give the signal to open fire on us.

"Any man worthy of your daughter would tell

you that she's priceless. Her soul is pure sunshine, and her strength shines through everything she does. No dollar tag can be attached to her."

My heart melts at his words despite the tense situation. He says the sweetest stuff about me.

The slight twitch of his left eye is the only thing that reveals my father is angry. He's spent too many years perfecting an excellent poker face to lose his shit now. "Fine. You have her. What will you give me in return?"

There's a whizzing sound and before I can even process what's happened, my father has dropped to his knees. His men aim their weapons toward the trees but there's nothing and no one.

Trace steps forward and kneels in the dirt with my father before Carl can get to him.

"Don't shoot," my father grits out the command, sounding pained. His words are met with nothing but respect as each man lowers his gun.

My mountain man says something in a low voice then pulls the arrow from his shoulder and helps him to his feet.

Fire blazes in my father's gaze as he glances at me. Blood trickles down his arm, and he's holding his shoulder at an odd angle. "You've clearly made your choice, and I will respect it."

Trace makes a noise, and my father quickly adds, "I will never darken your doorstep again. You have my word."

I don't say anything. I don't know this man making promises, and it hurts my heart.

My father nods to his men and they swarm around him, helping him into his vehicle. I watch the big SUV lumber back down the road until it's nothing more than a tiny dot.

I turn to Trace. He's busy talking with Roman, the two of them deep in discussion.

"Is that it?" I ask, releasing a breath. "Am I really free from him?"

He turns from his conversation to wrap an arm around my waist. "Yeah, you're free, sweet girl."

My knees buckle as relief flows through my veins. It's over. Trace and I are free from our pasts. We can move forward now. We can build a life.

Trace picks me up before I can tumble to the ground. He pulls me into his arms bridal style and calls over his shoulder that he'll catch up with Roman later. Then he's carrying me into our cabin. He settles with me on the couch, pausing to brush hair from my face. "You're free now."

Tears slip down my cheeks at his words. All of this stress I've been carrying for the past two weeks is rolling off my shoulders. We're free to be together.

He lets me cry, stroking my hair and whispering sweet nothings under his breath. He rocks me, comforting me with his presence and reassuring me that I'm safe now.

When I finally stop crying, he wipes my face and smiles down at me. Tenderness and affection are in his gaze. How did I get this lucky? How did I go from being a prisoner in my own home to finding the love of my life here on this remote mountain?

His words from earlier come back to me. "You called me your future wife."

His smile is soft. "I have the ring. I wanted to ask you tonight, but it slipped out when we were talking."

My heart is so happy that it feels like I could float away. This handsome mountain man wants to make me his wife. I cup his face, his beard soft against my palm. "For the record, I'll say yes."

"Doesn't matter. I'd drag you to the courthouse either way," he teases.

I laugh at his mock threat. This man would never make me do anything I don't want to. His every thought is about what I want and how he can provide it for me.

"I love you," he whispers.

"I love you, too." I lean up and press my lips against his, sealing our love with a kiss. For the first time in a long time, it's easy to breathe. I feel light and carefree. More than that, I'm happy. I'm in love with an incredible man and my future looks bright.

15

TRACE

I PACE UP AND DOWN THE STEPS OF MY FRONT PORCH, needing to feel my body in motion. There's been restless energy inside of me all morning as I count-down to the moment that I can finally claim Molly as my wife in front of all our friends and family.

We've been engaged for a month. I wanted to take her down to the courthouse the moment she slid the engagement ring on her finger. But she's already missed out on so many life experiences that I wanted to give her a proper wedding. Even if waiting for this day has been one of the hardest things I've ever done in my life.

Last week, I got the notice that I'd no longer be billed for the hospice service. Seems that my stepdad finally died. True to their word, no one from my family has reached out. Not that I expected them to. It's a relief to know I'm free.

Looking back, I see that both Molly and I had to face our pasts in order to find our way to each other. We spent our lives running, not knowing we were running toward a beautiful future. One that we get to experience together.

If I had to go through it all again just to get to this moment, this chance to be with her, then I'd do it in a heartbeat. She's been worth every moment of pain, loneliness, and despair. She was worth the wait and now I get to show the world that she's mine.

"Sit down somewhere. You're making the rest of us dizzy," Blade complains from his spot on the front porch. He's the one who shot Molly's dad with the arrow. How a one-armed man manages to shoot an arrow, I'll never know. Maybe next time I'll get the chance to watch him do it.

"He's just cranky because he's not writing a romance book," Rafe teases him. He, Blade, and Roman are sitting on my front porch in wicker chairs. Apparently, my porch needed a seating area, complete with throw pillows and a rug to "pull the look together". It amazes me how Molly came in and transformed my lonely cabin into a beautiful home.

"For the last time," Blade sighs, popping the tab

on a beer. "I don't write romance. I read them. Get paid for it too."

"How does that work?" I mutter, not even a little bit curious. I'm far more interested in seeing my bride today than I am hearing about Blade's work.

"I'm a book narrator. Romance books happen to be a billion-dollar industry, and I want my slice of the pie. It's about the money." He leans back in his chair and stares out at the horizon, like something is troubling him.

Roman snorts. "Sure, nothing to do with the pretty little author that keeps messaging you, wanting to meet up in person."

Blade's expression falls. "Yeah, that's not happening."

I remember how lonely I was just a few weeks ago, right before I found Molly. There's nothing like knowing I have someone to come home to at night, someone to talk with about my day, and cuddle underneath the blankets. "Maybe give her a chance. Don't reject a good thing before it can happen."

My phone finally beeps, signaling it's time and I breathe a sigh of relief. We can take our place for the ceremony where my beautiful girl will walk down the aisle so I can properly stake my claim.

We haven't heard from her dad since that day

when he met with us. I don't suspect we ever will. The man is a coward who wouldn't even fight for his daughter. He just saw her as a pawn, but he wasn't willing to risk his life for her. Not the way I would. I'd lay down my life for my bride without hesitation. She's my whole world, my queen.

Before we can move from the porch, Brennon and Nash are showing up. Brennon punched his brother in the nose at his wedding and took his bride for his own. Nash fell for a curvy little thief who broke into his home. They're both settled and peaceful since marrying their women. It seemed weird to me for a while, but I understand it now.

They offer their congratulations on the way to the wedding venue. Molly wanted to get married under the oak tree, the same one where we first made love. I can't argue with that. We often come here when the weather is nice to fool around.

Cadence, Brennon's woman, and Laura, Nash's wife, helped turn the forested area into a fairytale wedding. They brought Molly's vision to life and I'm glad that she has them.

The guys take their place with me by the tree as we wait for the women. We exchange pleasantries with Judge Helen. She does a lot of wedding cere-monies in Courage County and the ones she doesn't handle are usually down at the wedding chapel.

The organ music begins, piped in from the speaker system the guys rigged up for the wedding and my girl is coming down the aisle.

Princess struts down the path with her head held high despite the floppy hat. It's as if she understands the importance of the moment because for once she doesn't meow dramatically over my choice of music.

When she gets to my feet, I lean down and gently remove the wedding rings from her collar. It was important to both of us that Princess be part of the wedding. She's a part of our family.

She settles beside me just as Cadence and Laura make their way down the path. Then it's finally time for my woman. She practically floats down the path, her smile brighter than the sun.

My chest tightens as I make a silent vow to give her a million reasons to smile. Her happiness will always be my priority. I'll make sure she feels loved and adored every day for the rest of our lives.

When she arrives in front of me, I clasp her delicate hands in my own. She's been working with clay again. I set up a separate part of the workshop that's far enough away from my welding she's not likely to get hurt.

She enjoys having a dedicated space for her clay creations and I even ordered a top-of-the-line kiln. But I love having her nearby for selfish reasons. It makes it easy to sneak in and steal a few kisses when we're between projects.

We recite our vows. She's teary and I'm allergic to the damn pollen in this forest. That's why I'm blinking back tears as I repeat the words that will make her mine forever.

When I lift her veil, she beams up at me. "I love you, my warrior."

Every time she calls me that, I think back to our stolen moment in the store dressing room. She knows it too. It's her way of reminding me of all the fun things we'll do tonight as husband and wife. "I love you, my queen."

I lean down to kiss her, my heart overflowing with love for this woman. I can't wait to start our married life together.

EPILOGUE

MOLLY

"Have you seen my earring? I think I lost it in the bedding," I call over my shoulder as I pretend to search our big, comfy bed while bent over.

"No," Trace calls from the bathroom where he's brushing his teeth. My husband and I have been married for just over a year, and I love our life together. We spend our days in his workshop. Me with my clay creation and him on his welding. Although, we have spent the past six months collaborating on a very special project.

We worked together to create a special all-access park in Courage County. It's designed to be accessible to everyone, including families with mobility issues.

Designing it was something we both felt strongly

about after we watched our friend, Ranger Scott, growing frustrated when he was playing with his kids in the park. His power wheelchair made it more difficult for him to join their games.

After talking about it and coming up with a few rough ideas, we brought the concept to him a few weeks later. He loved it and gave us some great feedback. We also brought in Mallory Scott to hear her thoughts too.

Now the project is complete and it's opening day. I couldn't be prouder of what we've created, or the way Trace was so committed to getting every detail right. He even funded the park, though no one knows that but me. It's officially a gift from his foundation, carefully hidden under shell companies.

I stop pretending to search the bed and straighten, putting a hand to my back as I do. All of that time I spend stooping over to work on my pottery is taking a toll.

I might have to start my yoga videos again. But every time I do, Trace sits down and watches my workout. It's all of five minutes before he has me out of those yoga pants and on my back, stretching me in entirely different ways.

Shaking my head, I grumble under my breath to Princess, "He's not paying attention to me at all."

She meows as if she understands how frustrating the big mountain man can be.

When he moves into the bedroom to slip into his fancy blue dress shirt, I pretend to drop my phone under the bed. I don't really need one because I use his phone most of the time, but Trace insisted I have one in case there was ever an emergency when we're apart. That's pretty rare though. The two of us are usually doing something together.

"Oops," I say and bend over to grab it. I can still bend now. I looked it up. Totally safe for me to bend.

My husband must have noticed this time because he's finally across the room behind me. His finger-tips brush the bottom of my sleep shorts, touching the frilly edges. "You need something from me, sweet girl?"

"Yes," I answer unable to hold back my moan when he pulls down my shorts. Cool air rushes over my skin and his fingers probe my entrance. I already know he'll find me wet. So very wet and aching for my man.

We've spent a lot of the past year listening to sex podcasts, and it's done great things for teaching us how to communicate about what we want in the bedroom. We've learned a lot about each other and what turns us on individually.

"We only have a few minutes before we leave," he warns as he thrusts two thick digits into my aching pussy. He pumps his fingers, readying my body. He's still so big and getting me ready is the only way I can take him. "You're so wet, sweetheart."

"Kept dreaming about you last night," I explain as I reach for the foot of the bed. I bend over it, just the way he likes. My husband is an ass man. Nothing gets him going like seeing my ass in the air.

"What were you dreaming about?" He asks as he moves his fingers and aligns our bodies. He shoves inside in one quick thrust. I love it when he's a little rough with me.

"About this," I sigh in contentment once he's seated fully inside of me. It's so, so good. I thought our wedding night was the best ever—when he took me underneath that oak tree again. But he just keeps making it better.

"Mmm, tell me about your dream," he murmurs as he drapes his body over mine, pressing soft kisses to the back of my neck. This is what I love about him so much he's both tender and loving and dominant and rough. He always knows how to walk the line between the two.

"You were inside of me, just like this," I pant as he

continues to ram into me, driving his cock deeper and deeper.

"Was I playing with that pretty clit?" He growls.

"Yes!" I gasp out just as he reaches for mine. He circles the little nub, sending another wave of pleasure through my body.

"Was I telling you what a good girl you are?"

I'm practically sobbing now because it's so good. So many wonderful sensations at once. The way he's hammering into my pussy, rubbing my clit, and saying filthy things into my ear. All of it builds to a crescendo, and I barely have time to gasp out that I'm coming.

His release follows mine and he stills for a moment as he empties himself inside of me. I love the way it feels to have his warm come between my thighs. I love the way it makes me feel owned and possessed.

When he pulls out, he takes me to the bathroom and cleans me up. I'm sitting on the counter as he stands between my knees. After he's done, I see the sadness flicker across his face.

"Maybe this time," he murmurs softly. He wants a baby so desperately. We both do. We've been actively trying for over six months now. I talked to Summer about it. She told me that it can take up to a year to conceive the natural way and encouraged me not to give up hope just yet.

I was going to wait to tell Trace what I discovered while he was in the shower. I didn't even tell him I was taking a pregnancy test this time because it's always negative and it makes both of us so sad.

But it was positive and the moment I saw it, my heart fluttered in my chest.

I planned to tell him tonight after the grand opening. I didn't want anything to detract from his special project. He calls it our project, but he's put way more work and care into it. All I did was come up with the idea.

"Not this time," I tell him. "But another time."

He tips my chin up and presses a soft kiss to my lips. "You're right. We'll get there eventually. When the time is right."

My eyes mist over. They've been doing that so much lately and I finally know why. "No, you don't understand. We didn't make a baby this time because we already did. I'm pregnant."

He shakes his head like he didn't hear me. "You mean…we're…?" A slow grin crosses his face. He looks as happy as he did on the day we married each other.

"We're pregnant," I reassure him and grab his

hand. I place it over my tummy. Right now, there's not anything to feel. There won't be for weeks but just knowing our little baby is growing inside of me right now is filling both of us with such joy.

He runs a thumb across my stomach and bends low, talking to my non-existent bump. "Hey, little one. It's Daddy. Your mommy and I just want you to know how excited we are and how much we love you."

His voice breaks, and I put a hand on his face. The sheen of tears in his eyes matches my own.

He presses a kiss to my palm. "We're starting a family."

I smile back at him. "You're going to be an amazing father."

I know it's true too. Trace is already such an amazing husband. He provides for my every need. He protects me from everything, big and small. But most of all, he loves me completely. I know he'll love our babies just as fiercely.

Want a bonus scene with Trace and Molly? Sign up for my weekly newsletter and get the bonus here.

*Can this dirty mountain man convince the romance
writer he wants to be the hero in her own personal
love story?*

Blade

I'm the man that reads her dirtiest fantasies out loud.
Yeah, I'm a book narrator. I spend my nights reading
my favorite author's filthy words for her fan base to
listen in on. Every naughty scene only makes me
crave her more. But she can't know who I really am.

Then Gwen, the curvy goddess, shows up on my
mountain, looking for my alter ego. I figure I'll take
her around town and help her search. After she

finally admits she can't find him, I'll send her back. Easy and simple.

But when it's time for her to leave, I can't let her go. Maybe we can write a happily ever after of our own together.

Gwen

Every time I hear my book narrator's voice, I melt. I've been trying to draw him out for six months now, and he won't tell me who he is. So, I do something a little bit crazy. I take a trip to his mountain. If I can just see him in person, then I can get over my stupid crush.

Except I end up stranded with a dirty mountain man who's making me crave his fiery touch and his filthy mouth. Have I finally found a romance hero of my own?

If you love a dirty talking alpha male who seduces his curvy goddess, it's time to meet Blade in Romanced by the Mountain Man.

Read Blade and Gwen's Story

Welcome to Courage County where protective alpha heroes fall for strong curvy women they love and defend. There's NO cheating and NO cliffhangers. Just a sweet, sexy HEA in each book.

Love on the Ranch

Her Alpha Cowboy

Pregnant and alone, Riley has nowhere to go until the alpha cowboy finds her. Will she fall in love with her rescuer?

Her Older Cowboy

Summer is making a baby with her brother's best friend. But he insists on making it the old-fashioned way.

Her Protector Cowboy

Jack will do whatever it takes to protect his curvy woman after their hot one-night stand…then he plans to claim her!

Her Forever Cowboy

Dean is in love with his best friend's widow. When they're stranded together for the night, will he finally tell her how he feels?

Her Dirty Cowboy

The ranch's newest hire also happens to be the woman Adam had a one-night stand with…and she's carrying his baby!

Her Sexy Cowboy

She's a scared runaway with a baby. He's determined to protect them both. But neither of them expected to fall in love.

Her Wild Cowboy

He'll keep his curvy woman safe, even if it means a marriage in name only. But what happens when he wants to make it a real marriage?

Her Wicked Cowboy

One hot night with Jake gave me the best gift of my life: a beautiful baby girl. Will he want us to be a family when I show up on his doorstep a year later?

Courage County Brides

The Cowboy's Bride

The only way out of my horrible life is to become a mail order bride. But will my new cowboy husband be willing to take a chance on love?

The Cowboy's Soulmate

Can a jaded playboy find forever with his curvy mail order bride and her baby? Or will her secret ruin their future?

The Cowboy's Valentine

I'm a grumpy loner cowboy and I like it that way. Until my beautiful mail order bride arrives and suddenly, I want more than a marriage in name only.

The Cowboy's Match

Will this mail order bride matchmaker take a chance on love when she falls for the bearded cowboy who happens to be her VIP client?

The Cowboy's Obsession

Can this stalker cowboy show the curvy schoolteacher that he's the one for her?

The Cowboy's Sweetheart

Rule #1 of becoming a mail order bride: never fall in love with your cowboy groom.

The Cowboy's Angel

Can this cowboy single dad with a baby find love with his new mail order bride?

The Cowboy's Heiress

This innocent heiress is posing as a mail order bride. But what happens when her grumpy cowboy husband discovers who she really is?

Courage County Warriors

Rescue Me

Getting out was hard. Knowing who to trust was easy: my dad's best friend. He's the only man I can count on, but will we be able to keep our hands off each other?

Protect Me

When I need a warrior to protect me, I know just who to turn to: my brother's best friend. But will this grumpy cowboy who's guarding my body break my heart?

Shield Me

When trouble comes for me, I know who to call—my ex-boyfriend's dad. He's the only one who can help. But can I convince this grumpy cowboy to finally claim me?

Courage County Fire & Rescue

The Firefighter's Curvy Nanny

As a single dad firefighter, I was only looking for a quick fling. Then the curvy woman from last night shows up. Turns out, she's my new nanny.

The Firefighter's Secret Baby

After a scorching one-night stand with a sexy firefighter, I realize I'm pregnant…with my brother's best friend's baby.

The Firefighter's Forbidden Fling

I knew a one night stand with my grumpy boss wasn't the best idea…but I didn't think it would lead to anything serious. I definitely didn't think it would lead to a surprise pregnancy with this sexy firefighter.

GET A FREE COWBOY ROMANCE

Get Her Grumpy Cowboy for FREE:
https://www.MiaBrody.com/free-cowboy/

LIKE THIS STORY?

If you enjoyed this story, please post a review about it. Share what you liked or didn't like. It may not seem like much, but reviews are so important for indie authors like me who don't have the backing of a big publishing house.

Of course, you can also share your thoughts with me via email if you'd prefer to reach out that way. My email address is mia @ miabrody.com (remove the spaces). I love hearing from my readers!

ABOUT THE AUTHOR

Mia Brody writes steamy stories about alpha men who fall in love with big, beautiful women. She loves happy endings and every couple she writes will get one!

When she's not writing, Mia is searching for the perfect slice of cheesecake and reading books by her favorite instalove authors.

Keep in touch when you sign up for her newsletter: https://www.MiaBrody.com/news. It's the fastest way to hear about her new releases so you never miss one!